Project Ostium

Author: Gregory Guntren

Editor: Hannah Marks and Erin Guntren

2018-2020

Contents:

Preface

In 2018 after completing my first short novel, Conner's Reach: Whispers in the Wood, I wanted to start providing some original and more consistent content for my Patreon page. I saw Patreon as providing a great way to explore my writing techniques and style in a place where I could give content to my audience at a faster rate than authors are normally afforded. I started writing a horror story called Open Mind Hardened Heart. When I finished it, I saw an entire world of possibility created by that story. When I started Stalkers shortly after it, I realized that this was going to be a vast interconnected story and not individually contained stories like I had originally envisioned. The journey of Project Ostium has taken over a year to create and was only made possible by the editors and Patreon. A big thank you to all that helped make this possible. I am extremely proud of Project Ostium and am thrilled to have it all here in one complete form.

Project Ostium I: Open Mind and Hardened Heart

Nolan County, Missouri

Bill Manders released a deep sigh of contentment as he sat in his deer stand overlooking the wooded valley that cut through his property among the Ozark mountains. He gazed up at the clear blue-sky and knew he could not have wished for a better day for the start of deer hunting season. His breath lightly misted in front of him as the chill air bit at his face. His Remington shotgun was cold in his bare hands and the leaves had recently fallen allowing for a clear view up the valley and the creek that ran down through it. A light breeze gently shook the trees and carried a fresh pine smell that he took in deeply. He loved everything about hunting but most of all he loved the isolation. His kids always gave him a hard time about going out at his advanced age of seventy-two and he told them that he would rather die in the woods than go through life cooped up in his home collecting dust.

The sun started getting low on the horizon behind Bill painting the forest in a moody dark blue color. As perfect as the day had been, he hadn't seen a single deer all day. *Of course, a flock of turkeys went by, as would be his luck, in their off-season* he thought to himself light heartedly. He had leveled his gun on them and mimicked pulling the trigger. "Next time boys," he laughed softly to himself. He spit out the dip of chew he had been working on for the last hour and very carefully made his way out of his stand. Despite his constant reminders to his children that he is still young and agile, he was more than aware that he was too old to be falling out of a deer stand deep in the Ozarks.

Bill soon regretted waiting until the last inch of sunlight faded over the horizon to head back. He often did not account for the fact that he was moving slower these days and it was not long after he had gathered up all his gear and started off down the trail that darkness had completely fallen. The sky was clear, millions of stars shining bright, and a half moon had risen providing enough light for him to find the small walking trail that led back towards his home. The forest was silent beyond the sound of crunching leaves under his boots and the gentle babbling of the creek running alongside the trail. He was not afraid of the dark, but he did have a sensible fear of

the rare chance encounter with black bears or cougars.

The trail rose out of the valley to come into an open pasture

where Bill had once kept cattle years ago. As he reached the

pasture, he saw two lights off in the distance. "Who the hell?" Bob

whispered to himself as he clicked the safety off on his shotgun. He

knew it would be wiser to just let whoever it was trespassing move

on through but he just couldn't. Another aspect of age he found was

that people thought they could just walk all over you. *Probably*

damn teenagers thinking this old man's farm was as good as theirs

to poach on. Well fuck that, I am going to show them this is my land

dammit! he thought angerly.

Bill started across the pasture towards the swaying lights that

were a hundred yards in front of him. He had barely taken ten steps

when he suddenly saw movement to his left. He spun quickly and

caught a glimpse under the moonlight of a grey scaly creature with a

long tail rising and falling in the tall grass. Bill froze, rooted to the

spot as he watched it look back towards the lights. The face that

came into view shocked him. As it stood fully erect it was nearly his height. He could see it had leathery skin covered in bumps and ridges that reminded him of an alligator's back, with patches of pale fleshy skin scattered all over its body. The creature's mouth appeared too big for its skull as it stretched all across its face with jagged teeth showing as its mouth was partially open, panting. Bill found his gaze drawn to its large human-like eyes that stared at the lights with horror.

Bill followed the creature's eyes to the lights and saw they were heading off across the pasture away from them. He could hear the creature's shallow breathing and turned back to see that it was staring right at him. His heart froze in his chest. Only about ten feet separated the two of them and Bill knew that would not be enough for him to make a run for it. Now that it was fully turned towards him he could see the creature in more detail. It's arms were elongated and unnatural with human hands that had the scaly flesh and long claws at the tips of the fingers. The creature seemed an impossible mishmash of human and reptile parts; as if a mad surgeon had surgically cut pieces out of a human and sown lizard flesh to replace it. The worst part for Bill were those human eyes that stared at him. The sad, ruddy brown eyes that were filled with fear and pain.

Bill's own fear took over his brain as he slowly started to raise his shotgun on the creature. An understanding entered the eyes of the creature at the sight of Bill's gun, and it started to move towards him. The creature dropped down on all fours to crawl towards him in a sickening waggle motion that made it seem even more unnatural as stubby spines glinted in the moonlight on its back and a long thick reptilian tale stretched out behind it. Bill brought the shotgun to his shoulder and let fire a quick round but in his haste, he fired high over its back. He took a step back and felt his heel catch on a large rock and the world spun as he fell backwards, landing with bone rattling force.

Fresh panic filled Bill's mind as soon as he lay on the ground. He felt a heavy hand grip his leg and let out a shrill cry that he did not even recognize as a noise he could make. He sat up and the creature was now on both his legs moving up his body. It was heavy, pressing hard against him, and the wide shark grin on its mouth was open with a low gurgling noise escaping it. A thick fetid breath washed over Bill, causing his eyes to water. His right hand still gripped the shotgun and he brought it with all his force against the side of the creature's body. It tumbled off him letting out a low moan as it struggled to right itself. Bill brought the shotgun back to his shoulder and fired again hitting the creature directly in the chest, splattering him in hot blood.

It made one last effort to roll over to him, but only managed to roll on its side. Its sad human eyes looked into Bill's as they slowly glazed over. Bill limply scooted away from the horror before him. He could feel a tightness in his chest forming as fear and adrenaline filled him. He looked out to where he had last seen the lights in the field, and saw those two lights moving quickly towards him. He struggled to stand up, but the pain in his chest was keeping him from even catching his breath. He still held the shotgun and through the pain managed to get two more shells back into it. As the lights got close, he could hear voices behind them. "No, I think he did…Ah fuck he did!".

The two lights stopped before him and he could just make out the outline of two men behind them. Bill held up his left hand to shield his eyes from the lights that were some of the strongest flashlights he had ever seen. "It attacked me, what the hell was it?"

One flashlight clicked off and the man behind it knelt down beside Bill. He could see he was a young man, probably no more than twenty-five. The young man was wearing military style fatigues with a single badge on his left arm that Bill could not make out in the darkness.

"You fucked up big time old man. James! Check the Ascending One and see if it is dead." The light left Bill's eyes and moved over to the creature. James bent over it and tapped its head with the flashlight.

"He killed it. Well shit now what do we do?"

The soldier kneeling in front of Bill was only a dark outline against the star filled sky yet Bill could see a seething anger radiating from his eyes. The soldier reached out and grabbed the shotgun away and tossed it into the pasture. "You are coming back with us and you can explain this to the colonel."

Bill felt the tightness in his chest begin again and clutched at it as he started scooting backwards, pleading with them. "What the hell is going on? What is that thing?"

"That thing is beauty and transcendence. What happened tonight was a horrible mistake. A mistake we will answer for. I am ready to pay the price, I hope you are too." The man pulled a black baton from his belt and with a flick of the risk it extended out. Bill saw the baton rise to the sky framed against the stars. He could see now the symbol on the soldier's sleeve as the moonlight shined on it. It was an image of a golden door that was wide open with a blackness inside that was an abyss swallowing all light. Below the doorway one word was written, Ostium. He did not know the word but found he was transfixed on the darkness inside that golden doorway as if something was staring back at him from the badge. He became so fixated on the badge he did not notice as the baton came striking down across his temple. His body slumped over as he lost consciousness.

Bill awoke to searing pain in his arms as he was being dragged by a man on either side of him. He opened his eyes and saw the concrete floor below him and his legs stretched out behind him. A groan of pain escaped his lips as he struggled to lift his head to see down the narrow hallway. He saw a large door with red warnings emblazoned upon it at the far end. He tried to gain his feet but the men were dragging him too quickly for him to get his legs under him. The familiar voice of the man that had hit him spoke up, "We are close now. The colonel said we must go before the First. It is a great and terrible honor."

Bill could not understand what this man was talking about, but sensed a very real danger was beyond that door and he wanted no part of it. He started thrashing his arms and legs wildly with all of his strength.

"Be still, be brave. James are you ready?"

Bill could hear a soft weeping coming from James. *Dear God what is beyond this door that has one of their own breaking down,*

Bill thought in horror. James spoke and terror filled his voice despite a noticeable effort to hide it, "Yes…I'm ready."

They had reached the door. James reached out with a card that he scanned over a green screen where the door handle should have been. The sound of metal slamming inside the door several times echoed in the hallway and with a tremendous hiss of air the door opened a couple inches. No light could be seen or sound heard on the other side. Bill had stopped thrashing and hung limply as the door was pushed open before him.

A moist warm air escaped with a smell of rotting wood. The air stung his eyes with its intense stench. Bill looked into the endless darkness before him. A pair of red eyes appeared floating in the darkness, the black pupils of them were just thin slits that stared, cold and uncaring at him. "They call to me, in the dark of night. I will not turn away but look boldly forward. Open mind and hardened heart. Commit now to the way it was, so it shall be again." The two soldiers chanted the words in unison as loud as they could say them. The three men moved into the empty space, the ground wet and spongy beneath them. The soldiers started to repeat the chant over again as Bill felt the force of an unseen presence rush over him. His brain suddenly felt as if long claws were inside it digging and ripping at all he was, examining and prodding his very soul. The pain of this was beyond anything he had ever experienced.

Bill started to scream; his mind unable to process what he was seeing beyond the darkness. The door closed behind them and the locks slid back into place. All he could hear over his own screams was the chanting and then screams of the two young men. Then a single voice rose above the screams and Bill Manders was called to answer for a crime he did not know existed, committed against those he could not comprehend. As the voice continued Bill realized the truth he had not known. A truth that the voice promised all would know soon.

Project Ostium II: Stalkers

Ottawa, Canada

Cold air whipped around Charles Chenard, seeping through his black North Face jacket and blue jeans. His jet-black hair was unmovable in the wind as he kept it high and tight as he had during his service in the U.S. Marine Corp. He had kept it that way all through these last ten-years with the Central Intelligence Agency, despite the occasional backhanded comment from his peers. The frigid Canadian air did not bother him. He ran outside every chance he got to stay in shape and acclimate his body to the weather. He stood at the circular concrete vantage point that overlooked where the Rideau Canal spilled into the Ottawa River. He found this particular spot soothing as he watched the water gently flow by. He remembered hot summer days fishing with his grandfather off the boat dock outside Memphis. He had always held on to that memory as a place to go and be at peace. It had been years since he had returned home to Tennessee to visit his family. He did not regret this as he had grown to love Ottawa and see it as a second home.

Behind him the sound of crunching snow signaled the approach of his partner, Marshall Dunnett. Marshall, was a tall heavy-set man who had the soft look of someone who spent his days glued to a computer. He was impeccably clean and, despite his nerdy appearance, had no problem attracting women. As Marshall approached, Charles could hear his labored breathing. It had a rasp to it that made his own lungs hurt.

Charles turned to greet him, "Asthma acting up?"

Marshall gave him a weary look, "Wasn't until I had to hike out to meet you here."

"It's a beautiful spot. So, what's so important that we had to move our scheduled meeting up to today?" As Marshall approached, he slipped on the icy ground, but was saved by the lightning quick reflexes of Charles from a hard fall.

"Easy, easy. Where is the fire?" Charles joked as he righted his friend. All the relaxing thoughts he had had just a minute ago drained from him as he saw a troubled look in Marshall's eyes.

"What happened?" Charles asked gently, holding Marshall up by his arms as his friend gave nervous glances to the tree line behind them.

"Someone is following me. Lots of them I think."

"What are you talking about? Who?"

Marshall managed to gain his footing and with it his wits. "I don't know for sure but it all started after I intercepted a communication between the U.S. embassy here in Ottawa and an unknown location in the United States two days ago. The message caught my attention as it was using an old military code that hasn't been used since the Cold War. They must have thought no one would remember it."

Charles clapped Marshall's shoulder, "Well they didn't account for your steel trap memory and your love of weird ancient code formats."

Marshall continued, not acknowledging Charles's light-hearted compliment. "This morning I noticed I was being followed and that is why I called you here." Marshall looked over his shoulder again at the tree line, his shaggy black hair unkempt and falling in his eyes as his head whipped around.

"How did you even come across it?"

"I was monitoring the U.S. ambassador, Nathan McDaniel, as you had requested, for information coming out of his office on the new trade proposal with Canada. That was when I intercepted the message that came in using the old military code. Once I had decoded it I found it was some reference to a security breach in Missouri at a top-secret Army base. The message mentioned the security breach and then a civilian incident but it didn't go into details. But it was all in relation to something called Project Ostium."

"Project Ostium? That is a new one on me," Charles said.

"I looked up the word and it is Latin for doorway. Not exactly a very descriptive term. Then I really fucked up Charles. I called it into some Army contacts I have from awhile back and all the replies were strangely similar in telling me that it does not exist and that I should not inquire about it ever again.”

“You did what? Dammit Marshall! I have told you before, you have to run all external communication through me first!” Charles’s voice had risen and he quickly got it under control. Marshall was panicked enough. As he took a moment to look away from Marshall, to control his temper, movement in the tree line caught his eye. The trees were only twenty feet away and he clearly saw several figures walking amongst them.

“Marshall, you were right about the tail. I can see three men are shadowing us in the tree line.” Marshall gave another quick glance to the tree line and froze up. Charles grabbed his arm and started walking back down the path along the river towards his parked car. The parking lot was not far but it felt to Charles as if it had suddenly become a mile away as the three figures trailed them from the tree line. “They will most likely try and jump us at the parking lot so stay close and don’t run or talk unless I say so.”

Charles knew Marshall's skills were in ciphering and hacking, which Charles had grown to greatly appreciate over the last couple years of work together, but what he needed now was for Marshall to stay out of his way. He positioned himself closest to the tree line and kept the three men in his peripheral vision.

Charles slowly unzipped his coat and reached in and pulled out his Walther 9mm pistol from his shoulder holster and brought it out to be clearly visible to the unknown stalkers. As they got closer to the end of the tree line, and the sun started to shine more brightly lifting the shadows, he could clearly see them. Two men and a woman in civilian clothes. Despite their humble appearance they carried themselves in a confident and calm manner, betraying discipline from military training.

The stalkers, still in the tree line, were now close enough that he could see the tension on their faces as they prepared themselves for an attack. He didn't know if they were reacting to his gun or to the assault, they most likely intended to launch at them, and he did not care. He was prepared to kill them if they tried.

As Charles and Marshall reached the parking lot the three stalkers quickly walked out into the parking lot behind them. Charles positioned Marshall behind him as he turned around to face them and tightened his grip on his pistol.

"Stop!" shouted the tallest of them. He was a tall imposing figure with a clean-shaven head, wearing a thick all-black jacket that gave him a barrel-chested look belying the lean figure beneath. "Agent Marshall Dunnett, you were told to stay silent on the matter of the Project. I have been instructed to take you with us if you failed to cooperate, and you have failed." The unknown assailants slowly started advancing. Charles raised his voice to a loud commanding tone.

"We are agents of the U.S. government and will not be harassed or taken anywhere against our will. Don't take another step!" Everyone stopped moving as the bald man let out a short low whistle. He was within only a few feet of Charles and had brandished his own pistol. He sneered at Charles.

"Agent, we are servants of a higher power than any government. I would say in time you will learn this but you will not live long enough to see what is coming." He blew a high-pitched whistle from his mouth that stunned Charles's ears and suddenly they were all rushing him.

Charles's training took over as he brought his gun up to bear on the man before him. He was a few milliseconds faster at raising his pistol and fired a shot directly into the chest of the bald man. The direct shot to the chest sent the man flailing backwards, gun flying from his grip. The other two rushed him so fast on his left that they reached him before he could bring his gun to bear on them. In the space of a second, they were desperately grabbing his arms and neck sending all three of them falling to the ground in a painful heap.

Charles's vision blurred when his head slammed into the cold black top of the parking lot. He felt fingers wrap around his throat and desperate hands reaching for his pistol. His vision cleared and he could see both assailants' side by side on top of him. A blonde woman with a long ponytail was struggling to grab the pistol from his hand and the other was a slim pale man who had one hand tightly around Charles's throat as he pinned his other arm down.

Charles felt his strength giving out and the gun being pried from his hands when a deafening shot rang out. He felt hot blood splatter his face. He saw the pale man's face was a ruin of gore and bone. He let out a gasp of air as the hands strangling him let up as the pale man let go to feel the shattered remains of his face. Charles shoved the pale man back, sending an arc of blood spurting through the air as the man toppled backwards. Charles grabbed the blonde woman's ponytail and yanked it as hard as he could whipping her head back. She let out a yell of anger. She back handed him, her knuckles striking his temple. His vision exploded with stars but he quickly recovered, brought his right knee to his chest and kicked out directly into her face. The blonde woman went sprawling backwards. Charles rose to a sitting position and fired two shots hitting her in the throat and chest. The shocked look in her eyes quickly faded to a glassy stare as blood quickly flooded out of her wounds.

Charles got to his feet slowly, his legs shaking from the adrenaline rush. The bald man had just bent over to retrieve his gun and Charles suddenly found himself staring down the black barrel of it. He flinched as the trigger was pulled. The click of the trigger was all he heard, the gun had misfired. The bald man let out a yell of frustration and took off running back to the tree line. Charles was too startled to bring his gun up and watched as the man ran away.

"Holy shit!" Was all he could say as he looked at the dead in the parking lot. He had served his tour in war but had never been in a gunfight as close and personal as this. The fight had left him drained and he turned to see Marshall standing next to him holding a large silver pistol that was still pointed at the pale man's unmoving corpse. "Marshall? Marshall?!" He yelled to hear himself over the deafening ringing in his ear. Marshall jumped slightly and slowly lowered his gun.

"My God Charles, that happened so quick," said Marshall. Charles nodded in agreement. Marshall pointed after the fleeing man, "How did he survive that? How did you survive that?"

Charles shook his head, "He must have had body armor on, and I lucked out with his gun jamming, for sure. I need you to focus. We can't stay here another minute. We have to go." Marshall followed Charles to his white Sedan, walking calmly in shock from the violent event. They were quickly away, Charles drove as fast as he could to put distance between them and the canal area.

"Marshall what the hell have you gotten us into? Those guys meant serious business. There must have been more in that communication than you said." Marshall did not answer as he stared out the window, his body starting to shake as his adrenaline wore off.

"Marshall, I need you to snap out of it. You saved my life back there, that is what counts."

Marshall was roused by Charles's words and looked at him with large eyes, "I just did it. I wasn't even thinking." He fell silent and looked down at his hands still holding the gun.

"That man, he said they were servants of a higher power. What the hell does that mean? They had to be military, sent by our own military likely to silence you about this Project Ostium. What are we dealing with here? You have to know more."

"I wish I did. All that message said was a security breach had occurred at a military facility in Missouri. It was directed to Ambassador McDaniel, to pass on, but it didn't say to who."

"McDaniel? What would an ambassador have to do with any of that? None of this makes sense."

They drove on in silence until they were approaching the outskirts of the city. Marshall finally broke the silence, "Where are we going?"

"We need to regroup and figure out what our next move should be. I have a safe house up north just outside of the Mont-Tremblant National Park. It's out of the way and in the opposite direction of the U.S. where they hopefully think we'll flee too. We hunker down there and get in contact with the only person we can be sure to trust, Director Daren Washington. He is the only contact in the agency I trust one hundred percent."

Charles could see that Marshall did not share in his confidence. Charles knew if some covert branch of the military was after them then they needed allies. If Daren couldn't be trusted then all was truly lost and they might as well hide in the safe house until they were old men. They drove on in silence for hours, each man lost in his own thoughts, both sharing a feeling that their lives had reached a cliff that they were being forced to jump off of, into unknown danger.

Alexander Fortin stared up at the blue sky dazed. He had to take a minute to gather his thoughts as his eyes adjusted to the bright sunlight. Yells and screams filled his ears and his mind was jolted back to the fight. His years of military training allowed him to fight through the pain of being shot in the chest. His Kevlar vest had taken the bullet but the shock and pain to his body was still tremendous. A panic filled him as he realized those screams were his fellow soldiers, Rostov and Baker.

Alexander got to his feet just as agent Marshall Dunnett fired a shot into Rostov's face. His mind filled with rage at the horrible scene. He felt anger rise in him at his superiors who had assured him of the low threat target they were after; "a mere civilian" was their exact words. *That mere civilian is sure as shit a high threat now,* he thought bitterly. He had to struggle to catch his breath as the spreading bruise on his chest restricted his breathing. He looked around frantically for his gun on the icy black pavement.

As he bent to pick it up, he heard two more shots ring out and looked up to see Baker sprawled out on the asphalt, her blood turning the hard-packed snow red. He raised the gun at the man who had wiped out his entire team. Alexander aimed for the man's head and pulled the trigger. The silence that followed was startling as he realized his gun had jammed. A yell of frustration escaped his mouth and he quickly turned on his heel and ran. He knew he didn't stand a chance in rushing them and expected to be cut down as he ran. He was surprised when he reached the tree line alive. He did not stop to see what they were doing and was soon all the way back to the canal

unscathed.

Alexander did not stop running alongside the canal until he

reached an old white brick building with rusty red shutters. He ran

around to the side of it, slipping on the icy path and collapsed against

the side of the building. He unzipped his coat to let the hot air out

from under it. As he looked out across the park before him he saw

people panicking and running from the gun battle that had occurred.

The Kevlar vest was stifling hot but there was nothing he could do

about that as it was too bulky to remove here. He cleared the bullet

that had misfired then put his gun back in its holster.

His phone started to vibrate in his pocket. He knew it was

Command calling for an update. He contemplated letting it go, but

then dug it out of his pocket to answer. "Is it done?" said a cold and

distant voice.

Alexander took in a deep breath, then let it out slowly. The

adrenaline rush was wearing off and he felt his entire body growing

tired. "No, we ran into trouble."

"What kind of trouble."

"He wasn't alone or unarmed as we had been led to believe. They killed my entire team!" Alexander's voice had been rising as he spoke and he yelled the last sentence into the receiver. The voice responded, still cold but louder as the speaker spoke slowly.

"You failed to do the task at hand. You have let an individual get away that has information that could cause great problems for the Project. How is it you are alive?"

"I'm barely alive, I've been shot! This agent Dunnett had a friend that knew how to handle himself."

"I am sure it's all a very touching story but the reality is I will not be answering for your failure, you will. Return immediately to the barracks for debriefing." The speaker paused and Alexander thought for a moment that the call had been lost, but then he could hear a conversation in the background between several people. He got up and started walking back to his car as he heard sirens ring out in the distance.

"Are you still there, Sergeant Fortin?"

"Yeah, I am here."

"You have new orders. You are to report to the coordinates that I will message you. It seems it has been decided for you to fully realize the gravity of what your failure has caused. Be at the coordinates within the hour or you will find it hard to stay alive to see tomorrow." The call ended. The text came through shortly after that. Alexander looked up the location of his new meetup and saw it was at the U.S. embassy, here, in Ottawa. Was he finally being allowed into the inner workings of the Project? But he had failed, how could this be? He started jogging towards his car, prepared to face whatever judgement was to be laid upon him.

Project Ostium III: Terror in the Wall

Springfield, MO

Marcos Romano was afraid he was going insane. As he laid in bed staring up at the shadows cast on the ceiling, all he could hear was scratching from inside the walls of his apartment that was loud and unceasing. Marcos had first started hearing it a month ago. At first, he only heard the scratching at the military base he worked at. Yet as the weeks went on it had followed him home. In the tight confines of his three-room apartment the scratching was bringing him to the edge of madness. Scratches, always scratches. *Can the neighbors not hear it?* He shouted at them, pleaded with them to acknowledge it. Their only response was banging on the wall and shouts back for his silence. *Uncaring fucks.*

A smell had started to fill the room. A smell that brought back memories from his childhood. His mom had kept geckos in a terrarium in their living room. That smell was what was filling his apartment, the same putrid smell that would hit him when he opened the terrarium all those years ago, but this was more intense. *How could no one smell it?* "Can't you smell it!" he screamed. Loud violent banging on the wall was the only response. A siren roared down the highway right outside his apartment. *Maybe they are coming for the smell, it is so strong they must smell it too.*

Marcos, unable to sleep, watched the light of the sun's first rays brighten the trees outside the window of his bedroom. He had never appreciated such a simple thing until now. It was the normalcy of it. *There wasn't enough of that in this world of late.*

As he got ready for work, he tried to act as he did before this insanity. He brushed his teeth and put on his government issued overalls, fighting an urge to run out of the apartment as fast as he could. He did this all with his eyes closed to avoid the sight of what was occurring around him. The walls of his bedroom had started to tear open in long slashes. Inside the tears was a black emptiness, from which a strong breeze was escaping. The breeze was carrying the humid terrarium smell with it. Once he had his work boots on and laced a thought hit him. *I cannot go back to the military base. It is at that base waiting for me. What was waiting? Some madness*

"What is wrong with me?!" Marcos yelled and hit his head

with his hands. A knock at the door made him jump.

"Marcos? Are you in there? I have gotten another noise

complaint against you. Now I don't want to be mean but we need to

do something about this." The voice was his landlord, Mrs. Pierce.

She was a gentle old lady who had been one of the few people in

Springfield to make Marcos feel truly accepted since he moved in.

Marcos walked into the dark living room and opened the

door to see the diminutive and frail woman waiting patiently at his

door. The sun shined over the buildings in the distance, lighting the

parking lot behind Mrs. Pierce in a soft refreshing light. She smiled

at him but her eyes showed that she was upset. "Marcos are you

okay? You look as if you have not slept in days."

"I definitely feel that way. I am sorry for the noise Mrs.

Pierce, I really am."

"I'm sure you are dearie, but this is the third complaint this week. I'm afraid I have to get tough about it this time. I never want to threaten anyone but your neighbor, Mr. Almond, says he will start calling the police if I don't do something. He was afraid last night you had hurt yourself."

Marcos started to close the door slowly. "I have to finish getting ready for work or I am going to be late."

"I understand dearie, but we will have to talk when you get home tonight. Mr. Almond is not going to let this just go."

Marcos nodded in agreement and shut the door. He quickly went to his closet and pulled out a green gym bag. He started opening drawers and throwing their contents of clothes into the bag as fast as he could. The scratches continued, the large cuts in the yellow painted walls were now big enough to stick an arm through. The smell leaving the wounds in the walls was being followed by a musty humidity that was filling the air. He could hear a low breathing coming from the tears but refused to look directly at them. He was not going back to the base but he could not stay here or he was positive he would go insane. He had no idea where he would flee to but he had to get out.

Marcos zipped up the bag and ran out the door to his car. He tried to calm down as he fumbled with his car's key fob to unlock the car, accidentally setting off the alarm. He cursed as he turned it off and got into the car. The terrarium smells still stung his nostrils but the scratching was gone at least. He drove away, deciding to go north as far as he could before becoming too tired to drive. He had no destination in mind, just far away from Missouri.

Mrs. Peirce's concern grew as she watched Marcos run through the parking lot and drive away. When the door to his apartment had shut on her she had caught a whiff of something dead or rotten from inside the apartment. It reminded her of those true crime shows where everyone just ignored the strange man and the weird noises from his house and then it turned out he had dead bodies in there. She couldn't believe Marcos would be a serial killer but something was terribly wrong with him.

She got the spare key for his apartment in her office. She did not approve of breaking someone's privacy but she knew she would feel a whole lot better after a quick check. She quickly walked to his apartment and slowly opened the door. He had drawn all the shades leaving the room in darkness. The smell hit her in strength this time and brought to mind the zoo's reptile house. She could see a humid fog that was hanging in the air, making the apartment warm and damp. She slowly entered and flipped the light switch, but no lights came on. She stood for a moment at the door desperately flipping the switch up and down.

"Crap," she said and proceeded to open the shades to let the morning sun in. The living room was a mess of take out cartons and empty soda cans; however, this she expected of a bachelor and kept on walking. She went into his bedroom and saw the drawers from his dresser opened and their contents strewn about the room. She had her hand over her mouth to keep out the smell, gagging as she made her way through the mess. She started towards the window in the bedroom to let light in as the light switch in here also did not work. *Why had he not mentioned this problem?* She wondered.

She stopped halfway across the room when she noticed dark slashes on the wall. She walked up to them thinking perhaps he had cut into the wall to fix the power problem. *This is going to cost a fortune to fix,* she thought. There were dozens of slashes on the wall with a few big enough she could stick her head inside. They appeared to her as if a great bear had been ripping at the drywall.

As she drew closer to the biggest slash she could tell the zoo smell was coming from inside the wall, along with the moist air. She could hear an animal's guttural breathing followed by faint hissing coming from the opening. *Marco had never mentioned owning a pet before.* She looked inside and the space was deeper than it should have been; a vast emptiness instead of the two feet to the next apartment she had expected. As she peered in she noticed movement inside. She saw a figure standing what seemed ten feet away in the darkness. It appeared to be a hunched figure, manlike but off somehow. She started to call out to it when suddenly it started running at her in long loping strides. She could hear the hiss of a snake come from its mouth as it approached. She quickly pushed away from the wall, tripping over a pile of jeans beneath her. She did not wait to see if it reached the gap in the wall as she rolled over and ran out of the room for the front door.

As she turned left out of the bedroom she crashed into a man. She let out a scream as she was caught by him. She looked up and saw a familiar face.

"Mr. Almond, sweet Jesus you scared me! Quick we have to leave; something is in the wall!"

Mr. Almond let out a soft laugh, his six-foot figure towered over her and his large hands held her firmly in place. She could see the sunlight from the open shades glinting off his round rimmed glasses and an unsettling smile on his face. "Where did Marcos Romano go Mrs. Pierce? I saw him drive off in quite a hurry. I was just about to follow him, but you had to go snooping, didn't you?"

Mrs. Pierce started struggling as she heard the hissing and breathing in the bedroom growing louder behind her. It sounded as if more than one figure was in the wall now. "Please Mr. Almond you have to let me go! You are scaring me!" She started to cry.

"Oh now, shush, shush, shush, Mrs. Pierce. The rift will only be here for a short while longer with Marcos gone and no longer sustaining it. He has had such amazing power given to him and doesn't even know it." He had been talking in a mocking voice to her as one would talk to a baby. Yet, when he got to the last sentence his tone changed to that of awe.

Mrs. Pierce's mind raced as she tried to comprehend what was going on. She was sure that Marcos was insane after seeing the room, but Mr. Almond seemed to be just as insane. She struggled harder as he slowly pushed her backwards into the bedroom. She sobbed as her legs gave out and her strength left her.

"Oh Mrs. Pierce, look at it. I would love to join you but I can't. I have to find Marcos, it is too early for others to find out about all this, much too early. I know the First wants to come out but we must distract them from possibly doing that."

"What are you talking about?" Mrs. Pierce sobbed as she was pushed closer to one of the open gaps in the wall.

"The First. They are those who came before us. I am a servant for them. Look at them, oh how they writhe and struggle to be free. They have long been imprisoned. But as I said, it is much too early. In their current form they would wither and die if they got out." Mrs. Pierce felt herself being lifted by Almond off the ground, head first into the dark gap in the wall, his words became muffled as her head entered the gap. Once inside she saw only the dark outlines of forms moving above her. Hands of rough warm skin grabbed her head. She felt long claws close around her face and then the tremendous strength of those hands as she was ripped through the gap into the dark. She fell upon spongey earth. The sky had a dim white light shining upon it but she could not see the source. She felt sweat start to pour from her skin in the humidity that was ten times worse here than in the bedroom. Above her loomed several figures, reptilian shaped beings, yet with a human intelligence in their slit snake eyes.

"No, please." Was all she could say as they descended upon her tearing into her flesh with claw and sharp jaws. She was eaten alive staring up into a pale, empty sky.

Mr. Almond backed away from the rift and watched it slowly fade away. The long dark wounds slowly cleared up until no sign of them existed. He could hear the screams of Mrs. Pierce even after the rift disappeared, then that too faded. "Hear the terror of the past. It is a rumble in the chests of those that believe. A tremor to ripple around the world. Commit now to the way it was, so it shall be again." He chanted softly to himself. His favorite passage taught to him by the First acolytes. He felt blessed to have seen the glory of what was to come, several tears fell down his cheeks as he contemplated it.

He gathered himself and started back to his apartment. He needed to report all this and then he would have to chase Marcos. He packed up his belongings, lost in thought of all the wondrous gifts the First would bestow upon when he delivered Marcos to them.

Project Ostium IV: Decision Point

Charles Chenard could feel them chasing him. He was running through a featureless wasteland, the ground was dry, cracked earth, untouched by rain. The barren landscape was covered in an impenetrable darkness that hung heavy over the land. He felt weightless as he ran, without exhaustion, into the emptiness before him. The only sound reaching him was the heavy footfalls from his pursuers on the hard, dry dirt beneath his feet. The surrounding darkness felt like a comforting blanket of concealment around him, hiding him from the searching eyes of the unknown pursuers.

He was gripped with anxiety by the unrelenting pursuit, but comforted by a sense of his own strength and ability to deal with whatever was coming. He contemplated this duality as he rushed on to face an unnamed, unseen enemy that would leave him with only his innate abilities to deal with it.

He started to hear a strange noise in the distance. It sounded like a loud whistling as if from a factory that was signaling the end of a shift. He stopped running and held his breath to pinpoint the location of the noise. He struggled to see the source of the noise in the unending darkness, when a loud bang filled his ears.

Charles shot straight up in bed as he snapped out of the strange dream. He heard more banging that he could now identify as metal hitting metal. The sun was just starting to filter through the small cabin windows. Charles quickly slid his feet out of the warm quilted covers onto the cold oaken boards of the floor. His body bristled with goosebumps, his boxer shorts providing his only protection against the cold as he reached for his Walther pistol.

He slowly opened the door and looked out into the short hallway. Directly across from his room was the door to Marshall Dunnett's room. It was closed. Down the hallway he could see into the living room, but the kitchen was hidden to the left around a corner. He slowly started to make his way down the hallway, his pistol lowered but both hands on it, ready to raise it at a moment's notice. He froze as another bang came from the kitchen and he heard the irritated voice of Marshall coming from within. All the tension in Charles's body drained away. The old wooden floorboards let out a loud creak as he turned around.

"Charles, you up?"

Charles looked over his shoulder to see Marshall coming out of the kitchen holding a coffee can in his hand, "Why the hell are you naked and holding a gun?"

"I thought you were still asleep in your room," Charles said, slightly exacerbated by Marshall's question.

Marshall let out a loud laugh and went back into the kitchen cursing at the coffee maker he had been battling, "Pretty sure I'm going to kill it this time."

Charles didn't bother responding as he walked back to his room. He dressed slowly, trying to understand the dream that had gripped him so fully.

Both men sat at an old foldout card table that was the centerpiece of the kitchen. The cabin was Charles's run-down bachelor pad that was never intended to be lived in for more than a weekend. The guest bed was a discount air mattress that had led to constant complaining from Marshall. The walls were thin and the single bathroom had become a battleground over cleanliness and personal space. Going into their fifth day the meager accommodations were starting to wear thin on them. Luckily, friendship had always been easy between the two of them, but the cramped cabin was starting to bring out the eccentricities of each other.

Charles risked burning his mouth as he cautiously took a sip of coffee. He stared out a smudge covered window that gave a muddied view of the driveway, and the long road that stretched out away from them into the deep forest surrounding the cabin. Marshall was noisily chewing away on eggs across from him, a habit that made Charles's eye twitch, ignoring his friend as much as possible. He cautiously took a few more sips.

"Marshall this coffee is burned," He forced it down with a grimace.

"Well, feel free to make it yourself next time. I've been making it for days now and fighting your cheap coffee pot without a word of help or gratitude," Marshall choked down his own cup of burned coffee. "Also, the eggs probably got a little over cooked while I was battling the coffee."

He was just about to look down and see the damage down to his eggs when he saw a figure walking down the road. The lone figure cut a tall, imposing shape, despite appearing quite weary in stride from what Charles imagined must have been a long hike on foot.

"Someone is coming down the lane."

Marshall slowly turned his head to look out the window, "Maybe they are lost or had an accident?"

"Maybe," Charles slowly rose, "Whoever it is they are going to be here in a few minutes. Get your gun from your room then comeback and stand by this window. I will walk out and stop them so you can have a clear shot." Charles was proud of the effort Marshall had taken over the last few days to improve his marksmanship. Marshall had proven a quick learner, the memories of the fight in Ottawa still sharp in his mind helping to accelerate the training.

Marshall nodded quickly and took off to his room. Charles walked out the front door onto the small front porch and leaned casually against the side of the house. His hand rested gently on the pistol tucked into the waistband of his jeans. The figure walking down the road was clearly a man, taller than Charles and bald with a thick black jacket on. The man had his hands in his jacket pockets, his eyes staring intently at Charles as he left the paved road for the white rock driveway of the cabin. Charles stood up straight as he recognized the figure. This was the man that had survived the shootout back in Ottawa.

"Stop right there," Charles kept his voice as calm as he could. The bald man did exactly as he was ordered, his boots kicking out rocks as he came to an immediate stop. "Slowly pull your hands out of your jacket." The man gently brought both his hands out to rest at his sides.

Charles walked down the porch, keeping his pace slow as he made his way out to the bald man. As he approached, he brought his gun up to point directly at the bald man's head. The bald man leaned back with his hands now up, looking Charles square in the eyes.

"Give me one reason why I shouldn't put a bullet in your head right now," Charles said as he quickly scanned the tree line and down the road, but saw no signs of anyone else with the man.

"My name is Alexander Fortin and I am not your enemy."

Charles scoffed, "Last time we met said otherwise."

"I was just following orders, and we were not sent to kill anyone," Alexander saw Charles's eyes darting around. "There is no one else with me, I promise you that."

Charles locked eyes with him, "As if a promise from you means shit to me. How about you start telling me how you found me out here."

"Stop pointing the gun at me! I will tell you anything you want to know." Charles could see a defeated look in Alexander's eyes. The man looked thinner than the last time they met, his shoes and clothes were dirty and worn out. Charles lowered the gun and motioned for Alexander to walk to the cabin.

Charles followed behind Alexander and once inside the cabin motioned for him to sit on the couch. He called out to Marshall to join them from the kitchen. "Are you sure he is alone Charles? Why would he be here alone?"

Charles kept his gun down but did not let the tension out of his body, ready to put a bullet in Alexander without question. "Answer his question, why are you here?"

Alexander let out a deep sigh and started to roll up the sleeve on his arm. "This is why. They have given me a death sentence for failing them." Charles and Marshall looked in disgust at the blueish green scales that covered the left forearm and elbow of Alexander's arm.

"What the hell is that?" Charles exclaimed as he got closer to examine the arm.

"That is the real enemy," Alexander rolled his sleeve back down, a disgusted and ashamed look on his face as he did so, "It was that goddamned ambassador McDaniel. After I had fled from our fight, I was ordered to the U.S. embassy. It was there that they showed me the truth, and the end of us all."

Alexander hesitated as he exited his car in front of the U.S. embassy. The large glass and concrete monolith of a structure was imposing as he made his way inside. Several black uniform clad soldiers with the Project Ostium badge on their shoulders coldly

escorted him upon entering. One soldier held a nightstick in his

hand while a second removed Alexander's gun. Alexander knew he

was going to be punished as they led him on. He walked like a man

going to his execution.

Alexander's mind raced as they made their way to the top floor by

elevator. Had all his years of service been for nothing? He'd joined

the army with dreams of duty and service to Canada. Later, he

volunteered for Project Ostium. The promise of a great experiment

into soldier development drew him in. The mission was sold to new

recruits as a top-secret program to explore potential in soldiers

through advanced mental and physical enhancement techniques that

would lead to untold personal advancement and growth. Once inside

the project he, or anyone else for that matter, couldn't deny the

reality of the promised power when hearing of the astronomical rise

to greatness of Colonel McDaniel. The story whispered among the

participants in the program was that through Project Ostium,

McDaniel had become a super soldier capable of extraordinary feats

of mental and physical skill. The rumor was that he had stopped a

rebellion on a remote base single handedly with his new-found powers. He had created a military operation that connected the U.S. and Canadian armies into a singular mission to bring the two militaries to a greater global power. The man had eventually left the service to rise to the position of ambassador between the two countries to further this ideal of joint cooperation.

The elevator doors opened and one of the soldiers prodded Alexander in the back with a forceful stab of the nightstick. His dreams of becoming a better soldier and sharing in the mysteries of the project had fully faded as he entered the office at the end of the long white sterile hallway. He could feel an aura of dread permeating from the office.

Ambassador McDaniel was seated behind a large oaken desk, the curtains drawn behind him leaving only the fluorescent ceiling light casting a pale white light over the room. The room was mostly empty, except for two sparsely filled bookshelves, a grey file cabinet, and two dark stained, wooden chairs sitting exposed before the desk. McDaniel did not look up as he continued to frenetically write in a large notebook. A soldier gestured for Alexander to be seated as the door to the office was shut. He heard it lock behind him, trapping him in the room with two soldiers and McDaniel.

"Do you know what everyone's problem is, soldier?" McDaniel spoke in a deep voice that echoed in the room. McDaniel was dressed in a black military dress uniform; a black beret with the Project Ostium badge rested on the edge of the desk. A large hand reached up to scratch the short wiry hair that was left on his balding head.

"Sir, no sir," responded Alexander instinctively.

McDaniel slowly raised his gaze, his hazy blue eyes stood out in stark contrast to his black complexion. Alexander could feel McDaniel scrutinizing him, boring a hole through his head with his pitiless eyes. "They think we are the pinnacle. That we alone are masters of our world and our destiny," He paused for a moment, carefully considering Alexander before him, "Do you think you are special?"

Alexander was taken aback at the question. He looked away from the piercing eyes and down at the golden nameplate on the desk; Ambassador Nathan McDaniel was written in black against the gold plating on it. He gathered his wits, "Sir, I do not fully understand the question. I have never called myself special."

"Look at me," McDaniel said in a calm, commanding voice. Alexander met the gaze again and could see the hate in the man's eyes. "Yes, you do. You failed. The fact that you are still alive tells me that you see yourself as special. But soon you will realize there are powers beyond us that demand a great price for failure."

Alexander felt the urge to shift his eyes but fought it. He felt sweat start to run down his forehead. McDaniel stood up. Alexander rose with him, standing straight at attention. McDaniel walked around the desk to stand beside him, Alexander kept his eyes forward.

"Soldier, I am going to show you why we are not special." McDaniel turned around and stretched out his right arm. He started to slowly make slashing motions with his pointer finger extended out, dragging his finger towards him in a scratching motion. Alexander broke his stance to turn and look on as an electric charge filled the air, as if a thunderstorm was approaching. The hairs on his arm rose and he started to back away from McDaniel. An audible tearing noise filled the room, long black lines started to form on the floor before McDaniel. Alexander stared in disbelief as he struggled to process the impossible scene as the black lines merged and then started expanding out in an ever-increasing oval shape. Heat and

humidity poured out from the gap, choking Alexander with a terrible stench.

"Enter and you will see." McDaniel motioned for the other soldiers to push Alexander forward. Alexander was in shock as the soldiers slowly pushed him along the tiled floor towards the gaping void in the floor. As he neared the edge, he snapped out of his stupor and started to flail back against the guards. The guards overpowered him and shoved him bodily over the edge, and into the void.

Alexander felt his stomach rise to his throat as he fell into the void. He fell in, headfirst, but found himself exiting the void parallel to the ground, for a moment he felt frozen in the air before falling straight down on his left side, his shoulder taking the brunt of the fall. The disorientation left him dazed as he lay on the warm spongy ground. He fought a strong urge to vomit, closing his eyes tightly to force back sensation. The ground he was laying in was thick, sticky mud that clung to his face and clothes in large globs. The warm moist ground soaked through his clothes.

He rose to his feet on shaky legs that felt like jelly. The sky had a pale light illuminating it, but no discernable source for the light. He turned in place only to see marshland in all directions. The only visible features were withered, limp trees that dotted the marsh. A humid wind blew continuously across the marsh, bringing sounds of distant growls. His imagination began to run wild with images of monstrous beasts stalking the marsh. He frantically looked around for the opening he had fallen through, but there was no sign of it.

The thick air and muddy ground quickly left Alexander worn out as he slogged aimlessly through the landscape. The dead, gray trees grew denser as he marched on, soon forming a thick forest. In the marsh forest he felt the first sense of a presence following him. It started as a sensation of scratching at his mind, an alien experience that made him gasp in pain. As it grew stronger, incoherent images passed through his mind, places and events he had no memory of. He stopped and leaned against one of the dead trees, breathing heavily with sweat streaking down his body. The images were coming faster but with no more sense to them than before. In the foggy air behind him he saw a shadow approaching out of the gloom. It soon materialized from the fog and he stopped breathing for several seconds as it approached. The scratching on his mind was now a lance of electricity that filled his head with burning pain, he screamed in agony and passed out.

"I awoke to find myself being pulled back through a new black rift and into that office. I can't remember much else until I was dragged from the building and put into a Humvee."

Marshall and Charles had been staring down at Alexander on the couch for a half-hour as the man told his story, looks of disbelief and wonder on both of their faces. Marshall collected himself first and rolled his eyes, "How are we supposed to believe such a wild story? Charles, you can't believe this?"

Charles stared at Alexander who was resting his head in his hands, exhausted, "How did you escape?"

Alexander slowly lifted his head, "I told you I passed out. I imagine McDaniel pulled me out."

"No, not from this other world. How did you escape from this Humvee they put you on?"

Alexander leaned back and let out a great blow of air, "That is probably going to be even harder for you to believe. I was riding in that truck for a good hour when suddenly, we came to a stop. I heard words exchanged outside then gunshots. The two guards in the back of the Humvee with me, jumped out and more gunshots were fired. A short while later three men appeared at the door and told me to get out. They gave me your location and told me to run.”

"Well, that was convenient,” Marshall said sarcastically. Charles reached out to Alexander and rolled up his sleeve. The scaly skin on his arm felt rough and warm to the touch. Charles grasped tightly on to Alexander’s arm and reached into his pocket for his Old Timer folding knife. “What are you doing!?” cried Alexander. Charles did not respond, but flipped out the blade and cut a shallow line along the reptilian flesh, dark red blood poured out as Alexander let out a grunt of pain.

"It’s real, Marshall,” Charles said matter-of-factly as he stood back up. His hand shaking slightly as the reality that Alexander was telling the truth hit home. Marshall was speechless as he watched Alexander pull his shirt sleeve over the wound.

"So, what is it then? What caused that?” Marshall said with suspicion still in his tone.

"That is how we are all going to die. That is the gift being promised. The last thing McDaniel said to me before I left the room was, 'Now you have joined the First. Let your body be born anew.' I didn't know what he meant until a few hours later when this started to show. I…I can feel it spreading, I can feel it taking over." Alexander grew quiet and lowered his head again.

"Marshall. Kitchen. Now." They went into the kitchen, Charles angled his body to keep Marshall and Alexander in his vision at the same time, unwilling to risk taking his eye from Alexander for a second. He took a deep breath then whispered, "I believe him but what is happening to his arm is beyond me. Thoughts, ideas, anything, hit me with it."

Marshall stared at Charles with bewilderment, "Fuck I don't know, man. I was sure they had given him some kind of drug to make him trip but this is beyond that. It is like he has some kind of disease."

Charles shook his head, "I think it is something else. Though I had not considered contagion. Shit, and I touched it." Charles started to rub his hand nervously on his pant leg. A loud buzzing sound went off, it took Charles a second to realize it was his burner phone in his pocket. He pulled it out and saw on the screen the number of CIA Director Daren Washington. He clicked the bright green phone image on the screen, "Agent Chenard, go."

"Is he there? Did the Canadian soldier make it?"

"How do you know that sir?"

"Because we rescued him."

Charles felt a sense of relief fill him as one piece of the puzzle snapped into place. "How much can you tell me about what is happening, Sir? I'm operating in the dark here."

The silence that followed the question started to replace his relief with doubt. He was used to secrets being held close in this business, but he did not tolerate it when his life was on the line. "Tell me something, sir."

Director Washington's voice returned but softer, conspiratorial, "We have been working for several years to infiltrate Project Ostium. It started operating in Canada a few years ago. It's focused on communications with an unknown entity they refer to as the First. That is all I can say for now."

Charles suspected that much had been left out, but wondered if he now knew more than the Director after having heard Alexander's tale.

"What are we to do now? If you know Alexander's location, I find it hard to believe he has completely slipped from this Project Ostium's gaze."

Washington spoke in a weary tone, "I agree. Which is why I need you to leave immediately and return to the U.S. You and Agent Dunnett are two of the few field agents I can be one-hundred percent sure are not compromised, due in part to the attack you survived. We are tracking another employee of Project Ostium that worked at the main military base of the Project, located somewhere in Missouri. This employee has gone AWOL. Once you have crossed the border get in contact with me, and I can put you on their trail."

Charles was stunned, "Sir, I can't just walk through a border checkpoint with this guy. That leaves me illegally crossing the border with this Canadian soldier that is being hunted and then linking up with another hunted employee? Sir, with all due respect we will be a giant moving target."

"Yes, but I have few I can trust. The border is poorly monitored, you should have no trouble crossing. You have no idea how quickly everything has become compromised. The FBI is also hunting for this man, but I can't trust them either. No, it must be you. I have another agent that you will meet up with, and from there we can separate you all, and get everyone to safe houses. For now, just get out of Canada. I fear you do not have much time." The call ended before Charles could respond.

Charles slid the phone back in his pocket and stared at Alexander for several seconds in silence. He could feel Marshall practically exploding with questions, but walked past him and back into the living room, to kneel down on his heels before Alexander.

"Looks like we are stuck together for now. All our lives depend on us cooperating together. Do you understand me? You make one wrong move and I'll kill you without question or warning. We leave for the border in ten minutes." Alexander gave him a cold, tired stare as his only response.

Marshall came into the room but kept a wide berth from Alexander. "What did the Director say? When are we handing this guy off?"

"We aren't."

"What!? Why the fuck not."

Charles replied, "Because they want us to drag him along with us. We are going to go back to the U.S. and meet up with another runaway. But right now, we are getting the hell out of here before this guy's friends show up and murder us all. I suggest you get packing."

Marshall threw his hands up in frustration and walked down the hall, muttering curses the entire way. Charles understood his anger, but orders were orders. He looked back at Alexander and wondered what any of this meant and how such a story could be believed, even with the strange scales growing on the man's arm.

His mind drifted back to the strange dream he had. Was it prophetic? Were they all to be on the run from this black Ops organization that would end up hunting them to the ends of the earth? He rubbed his head where a severe migraine was forming at the temples. "Fuck, I am tired." He mumbled through the growing pain. Alexander continued to sit with his head slumped forward, staring at the floor. Charles felt pity for him, but knew as the stress of the situation grew, killing him was going to seem more and more attractive. He left the dark thoughts behind as he made Alexander follow him to his room to pack up his belongings. "How about you tell me your story again while I pack. I don't want to have missed a thing." Alexander nodded wearily and began his bizarre tale again.

Project Ostium V: Worlds Collide

Marcos Romano was feeling the effects of a nonstop twelve-hour drive. The sun had fully set leaving the world around him only lit with headlights and the dim ruby lit street lights lining parts of the interstate. He found himself struggling to keep his eyelids up and focus on the highway before him as he slowly started to veer off into the shoulder. The sound of rocks kicking up from the tires and the jarring rumble strip shaking his car snapped him back awake. He jerked the wheel hard, overcompensating, sending his car flailing back across the two-lane highway. His car's right-side tires digging into the loose gravel on the other shoulder and hitting its rumble strip. He gritted his teeth as he fought to straighten his car out and get it back on the road. He finally leveled out and let out a sigh of relief, cursing his own drowsiness. He looked in the rearview mirror and saw the headlights of several cars falling back to avoid an accident with him.

"Come on man, wake up!" He exclaimed and gave himself a slap to try and raise his drooping eyes. Fear was the only force moving him forward, but it was the only force he needed. He had fled his apartment in Springfield, Missouri earlier that day in a desperate bid to escape a waking nightmare. As he drove on north along straight interstate roadways, he had tried to think of some reason for this nightmare existing. The last month was blurring together in his mind. He knew it had started while working at the military base, deep in the lower levels of it, as a janitor. He remembered standing in a long white hallway, his mop running smoothly over the tiled floor. The hallway had hit him as a strange place immediately as it only had one door in it, a large steel door that stood at the far end of it with red stickers stating *BIOHAZARD/TOXIC CONTAMINATION* and *DO NOT ENTER* written on them. He had only given it a brief glance but as he did something changed. A static charge had filled the air and he felt a sudden migraine begin.

Sweat beaded Marcos's forehead as he remembered the moment, it had been sudden and uneventful at the time, but over the next several weeks a dread had built inside him. He wasn't sure when the smell had started but he could remember the day the scratching had begun. He was in the hallway again, buffering the floor when it slowly started to occur. It appeared to echo in the hallway, and then inside his mind. A sound of long claws dragging across ripping cloth and Velcro. It always filled his head when he was there or sitting in his apartment. His car had been his only bastion from the noise.

When he had woken up that day it had all come to a head. He felt bad about leaving his landlord Mrs. Pierce without giving a reason for his sudden departure. He simply felt that he had to get out and away, far away to escape what was filling his mind. The only destination that could come to his mind was his parents' house just outside of Buffalo, New York. It had only been a little more than a month since leaving but it might as well have been a lifetime to him. He'd had a lot of fights with his parents over jobs and money since he had turned thirty and was still living in their basement. His parents were older, having had him when they were in their forties, and he had told himself he stuck around to take care of them. It was a lie he had nearly started to believe, using it to avoid making meaningful relationships or trying for more schooling to get a "real job" as his father would say. He wasn't sure what their reaction would be when they saw him crawling back after only a month, but he was damn sure it would be better than the hell he had been living and breathing in Missouri.

His car's gas light came on just as he passed through Cleveland, Ohio. He pushed on for a few more miles then pulled off on an exit and into a small four pump gas station. He stepped out of his stale smelling car into the icy air blowing off of Lake Erie. The moon was shining bright in the sky with its cold light that did nothing to help against the icy breeze.

He stood at the pump, listening to the gas chug greedily into his car and reflected on that scratch that was not there. *Had he truly outrun it?* He did not know for sure but felt the first bit of hope enter his mind in a long while. It was soon replaced by the uncertainty of how his parents would act when he showed up on their doorstep. He had forgotten his cellphone in his haste to leave, giving him no way of easily reaching them. "Probably for the best," he muttered to himself. This way they would be unable to tell him no when he arrived, it would be too late for arguments, hopefully.

Cars and people flowed in and out of the gas station. He watched the myriad of people as he stood by his car, jealous of their normal lives and how they all seemed to have their lives together. The sound of the pump clicking off brought his mind back to the task at hand. As he pulled the pump out his eyes caught sight of a tan station wagon that had just pulled in and was parked in front of the store. It wasn't the car that captured his attention but the man inside. The bright gas station fluorescent lights illuminating an odd man with round rimmed glasses staring piercingly at him. The man's gaze had locked on to his own the minute he pulled in.

"Mr. Almond?" Marcos said softly and quizzically to himself. His mind raced to process what he was seeing. Had his often-annoyed neighbor, Mr. Almond, followed him for twelve hours straight? He couldn't believe such a coincidence had occurred that they both left and arrived several states away at the same gas station. Maybe Mrs. Pierce asked him to follow Marcos? He decided that made even less sense. He had only talked with Mr. Almond when the man was at his door telling him to keep quiet. He didn't even know his first name. These thoughts continued to jumble in his disoriented mind as he watched Almond leave his car and start walking towards him.

"You sure do drive fast, Mr. Romano. I thought you were going to crash back there for sure," Almond smiled at him but no amount of friendliness or concern showed in his eyes. Romano found himself locked in the gaze of those pitiless blue eyes. He was thankful that his car was between them, but even that felt like a flimsy barrier. He was unsure why he felt fear enter him, but he was now very sure this was not coincidence.

"I got a little tired, it has been a long drive. Did you follow me?"

The smile never broke from Almond's face, "I think that is obvious. Mrs. Pierce was very concerned, though I'm sure she is over that now." Mr. Almond gave a laugh, short and tittering. The laugh reminded Marcos of a child who had broken something and found the attention and anger of their parents funny. A chill ran up his spine.

"Well, you can go back. I'm fine. Actually, I should probably get going," He started for the driver side door. Almond ran around the car in a frenzied motion that startled Marcos, slamming the door shut as Marcos opened it. An intensity was in his eyes, the smile was gone.

"No!" He shouted, a shaking anger entering his voice. A couple walking by startled at Almond's shout, moving quicker to their own car. The anger that showed quickly faded away as he leaned in close to Marcos, a look of desire on his face, "You don't know what you have, what you are. You have been chosen, Marcos Romano.

Chosen by them above all others." Almond reached out and touched Marcos's shoulder, squeezing it firmly. "I was sent by the Project to watch you, bring you in if necessary. But I'm taking orders from a higher power now. A power that wants you to harness your gift. Let me help you."

Marcos tried to shrug off the iron grip on his shoulder but was held fast in place. Almond reached out with his other hand and touched the side of Marcos's head lightly. A static charge shocked his head. Marcos reflexively flinched away from the shock, sending his body slamming into the side of the car, the iron grip of Almond never loosening.

"Marcos, open your mind to it. Hear them. They are just out of reach for you. I felt the taste of it back in your apartment. Now, let your power go." Almond's iron grip relented, sending Marcos sprawling to the gasoline stained concrete. Almond loomed over Marcos, a shark smile splitting his face, hunger and lust glowing in his cold eyes. "Feel the First rise inside you."

Marcos heard the scratching start to rise up all around him. A heavy taste of ozone filled his mouth as he felt the scratching turn into a great tearing sound. The ground beneath his car opened suddenly in a wide black chasm that swallowed the entire car in the blink of an eye. Screams filled his ears from onlookers witnessing the sudden insane phenomenon. A great rush of hot humid air escaped the yawning chasm. Marcos's eyes went wide with shock at the sight. He scrambled to his feet away from the abyss before him.

"They rise!" shouted Almond, who had his arms stretched out in a welcoming embrace of the foul air. The sound of a great hissing escaped the rift followed by a pair of clawed hands reached up from the rift, grabbing the edge. Marcos was frozen with fear as he watched a man shaped reptilian creature start to pull itself up. A lizard face with a short snout filled with rows of dagger teeth grinned back at him. Two black oval eyes peered out from the reptilian skull starring hungrily at Marcos. He felt a scream rise inside him but only a coughing sputter escaped his lips.

The gas station was now filled with screams and the squealing of tires as people scrambled to flee. Almond turned to Marcos, "What wonder! What glory you have!"

"No!" Marcos finally managed to scream out and the great yawning void slammed shut slicing the reptilian horror in half. The hungry eyes never changed as the beast's upper half slumped forward, blood and gore pouring out on the concrete.

"What are you doing? Let your power flow, do not deny it." Almond said.

Another great rift formed to Marcos's left as he tried to understand how he had created the first one, then another, and another; soon he was seeing rifts opening throughout the parking lot, swallowing cars and people alike. He turned his face away from it all, sweat streaming down his face as he struggled to focus and deny the dozens of rifts in existence.

Marcos opened his eyes to see the rifts had closed again. The empty store front and parking lot almost allowed himself to believe they had never been there, but the dead reptile corpse just a few feet from him drove home the reality of what had occurred, along with the screaming clerk that was standing at the gas station door struggling to lock the door in a futile effort to keep the insanity out.

Almond was only inches from his face, "You have the power to do it at will. Lesson learned." He reached out to grab Marcos. Marcos was too tired and drained to resist, whatever force inside him that had opened and closed the rifts had left him feeling as if he'd just run several miles at a dead sprint. His head was spinning from the stench in the air and the quickly decaying reptilian beast before him. The flesh of the beast was melting from it as if the world was rejecting the reality of its existence.

Almond's tan station wagon was the only remaining car, a lone survivor of the great exodus. Marcos was roughly pushed into the back seat, his legs and arms unable to resist as every muscle ached and felt like jelly to him. Marcos's eyes were growing heavy as he struggled to stay awake. He laid his head against the top of the back seat and stared out the back window as the engine turned over and they started to back out. He noticed a pair of headlights parked alongside the road with several figures, illuminated by the moonlight, the people inside the car were pointing at him and debating with great gestures amongst each other. He lost sight of them as Almond backed up and started pulling out into the dark street.

As they drove away Marcos suddenly felt his entire body fly forward and into the opposite door with his face smashing into the window. The loud crunch of metal on metal had filled his world and set his teeth clenching together. The car engine was making a terrible clicking sound and he could hear Almond screaming at him and someone else as he crawled into the back seat with him. He turned his head, feeling the muscles twinge with pain, and saw the front of a white sedan was pushed against the side of the station wagon, the car he had seen must have rammed them the minute they turned onto the road. Three men had exited the car, two carrying guns, shouting loudly for them to exit the car.

"Move! Move! Move!" Shouted Almond at Marcos over and over again as he opened the door and pushed Marcos out into the road. Marcos tumbled into the road and rolled into the cold wet ditch, freezing mud covering his face. Marcos was more tired than he could imagine but upon seeing Almond's enraged face, Marcos felt a last bit of energy fill him. He gathered up his own rage and focused on the scratching in his head to imagine a rift. He imagined a small oval shaped rift just behind Almond in the road. As he did this he leaped up, and with every last ounce of strength remaining drove his head and shoulder into Almond's stomach. Almond's stomach was a wall of tense muscle that at first did not seem to give, but as Marcos pushed off with his feet, digging into the cold mud and grass he made those muscles give.

Almond let out a great wheeze of air and tumbled backwards into the road, vanishing as he fell to the ground. Marcos saw the dark emptiness he had opened up that had engulfed Almond. The warm air heated the mud on his face, making it run down his neck. He was falling forward into the hole. Almond had landed and was staring up at him, his eyes filled with rage and desperation. Marcos closed his eyes and imagined the asphalt of the road. He felt the asphalt hard and rocky upon his face and hands as he slammed into it. The rift had closed instantly.

Marcos laid on the ground in shock listening to the three men shouting at each other and him. He slowly rolled over and saw his saviors. The two with guns were kneeling over him trying to speak to him but a ringing had started in his ears that did not stop. Marcos reached up to his ears and shook his head to try and convey his deafness. He could make out by the lips of one of them that he was asking if he was okay. The man had a hardened face of a survivor of several life and death events in his life. This gave Marcos comfort that they may be police or detectives, though how they knew to help him was a mystery.

Marcos tried to say he was okay but felt the world grow grey then black as an intense urge to pass out took over. He saw the concerned looks on the faces of the hard-faced man and his softer, pudgier friend as they tried to rouse him. His eyes were losing focus and the last thing he saw was the third man, severe and intense, staring at him from over the pudgy one's shoulder. The look on his face was not so different from the awe and wonderment he saw on Almonds face when he had unleashed his power. A fear of this man entered him that made him want to stand up and run as fast as he could, but the darkness overtook his mind as he blacked out.

Project Ostium Part VI: A Call to Worship

A white sedan sped down an empty highway swerving slightly as the driver looked to the skies. Black helicopters passed overhead, flying low over the tree tops and houses with search lights beaming from under their cockpits. The sedan's headlights switched off, the driver slammed on the brakes and abruptly turned off the two-lane highway and into a rundown residential district. Only the street lights and a few porch lights provided any illumination to guide the driver's way as the sedan cruised down the street.

"Come on, man. Slow down!" shouted Marshall as he gripped the door handle and dashboard.

"Shh!" Charles said, holding a cellphone to one ear and the steering wheel with the other. "Sorry, sir. Can you say that last part again? What street?" He said calmly into the cellphone. Marshall didn't let up his death grip of the car but kept his complaints to himself, positive they were going to slam into a parked car along the street at any moment. He knew Charles was an excellent driver but with the headlights off in the dead of night, he felt all bets were off.

Charles squinted his eyes as he navigated the narrow streets, struggling to see street signs in the dark, and slowing down as he approached one then speeding up as it showed to not be the one he wanted. He heard another helicopter fly over and the street in front of him lit up from its spotlight.

"Are you sure these army helicopters don't know which way we went? How do we know the safe house isn't being staked out?" Marshall asked.

Charles ignored Marshall's questions, even though those very same concerns were running through his own mind. He spoke into the phone, "Director Washington, I just passed Newburg Street. I still don't see this Meadows street. Oh, wait. Yep, that's it." He slowly turned right. "On my left? Okay, looking now." Charles leaned towards Marshall, "He says the safe house is a one-story brick house with a large maple tree right in the middle of the yard."

Marshall muttered, "Great info, like I can see shit in the dark." He leaned forward looking intently at the houses despite his grumblings.

"There, two houses down," Alexander said from the back seat behind Charles. Charles saw it and pulled over on the opposite side of the street.

"Okay. Alexander, you stay in the car with our guy. Marshall, let's go check it out." Marshall gave an unsure look at Alexander who stared back at him blank faced. Marshall put on his best intimidating face, a long scowling frown, but seeing how unphased Alexander was he quickly looked away and followed after Charles.

Alexander watched them cross the street and disappear into the night around the back of the house. He turned to the unconscious man they had rescued. The man looked young, probably late twenties he guessed. He thought back to when they had crashed the car and seeing this man suddenly open a rift. It was similar to what Ambassador McDaniel had done in his office, but this guy had done it with far less effort. He had opened it without so much as a gesture. *How the hell was that possible?* He reached behind the man and slowly pulled out his wallet. He found a driver's license and a military ID that designated him as a civilian employee. *Not even real military? He can't be part of the Project then? Yet, he has the power.*

Alexander read out loud, "Marcos Romano, looks like your thirty. I was close." Marcos started to wake, his eyes still thin slits as he peered bleary eyed around. Upon seeing Alexander seated next to him he quickly woke fully and pressed his body violently against the door, trying to put as much space between them as possible.

"Where are the others?" Marcos asked. His eyes were wild with anxiety.

"They are scouting out a safe house for us for the night. Seems you attracted a lot of attention very quickly. Glad you woke up, wasn't looking forward to carrying you inside." He tried for a smile despite not genuinely feeling the humor of his own words. Marcos's eyes darted around, giving only furtive glances towards Alexander.

"Who are you guys? How did you know to rescue me?"

Alexander let the smile fall from his face. "They are CIA agents. They got a tipoff on your location from other agents. Lots of people seem to be monitoring you. As for the last question, well, you tell me."

Marcos, seeing his wallet open in Alexander's lap, reached out and snatched it back. Alexander put his hands up defensively. "Just wanted to know your name."

Marcos gave the wallet a quick look over. Once he was satisfied nothing was taken, he stuffed it in his back pocket. "You didn't answer my first question. Who are you?"

"I'm Alexander Fortin. I'm with the Canadian Army, well, was. I am part of Project Ostium. Same as you." Marcos's entire body went rigid with fear. Alexander could see he was getting ready to bolt. "Guess I should say I'm a former member of that, also." A sudden sullenness passed over Alexander and his face dropped even more as a memory resurfaced. He pushed the memory aside and said, "How can you do it? I have only seen one other with that power."

Marcos's hand fumbled for the door handle behind his back. He gripped it but did not pull, "Who?"

Alexander raised an eyebrow to him. "*Who?* Seriously, how can I have worked at the base and not know who?"

"I was just a janitor. I'm not a part of the Project. I don't even know what this Project is." Marcos saw two figures walking back towards the car out of the dark. Alexander let out a disbelieving laugh.

"A janitor? Don't lie to me."

"I'm not a liar. I only worked there for a month buffing floors and cleaning bathrooms."

Alexander pushed back the sleeve on his left arm, thrusting the arm out towards Marcos and said, "Look, look at what the Project can do. I know everything, so drop the bullshit. Tell me exactly how you got those powers and why." Marcos was unsure exactly what he was seeing at first. Alexander's arm was covered with blueish-green scales that glinted in the red streetlight. The only human skin left was on the hand and it had turned a pale blue. Marcos's mind flashed back to the reptilian monster that had climbed out of the hole in the ground back at the gas station. Its flesh was not so different from this man's arm.

He pulled hard on the door handle and tumbled backwards into the street landing hard on his back. He heard Alexander shout out at him and saw him crawling over the seats to reach him. A more distant shout gave Alexander pause before he could exit the car on top of Marcos. "Get the fuck back." Marcos looked up and saw the pudgy man from his rescue standing over him pointing a large silver gun into Alexander's face.

"Marshall, hold up. Don't shoot." came the voice of the military man he had also seen, "Get back against the other side of the car, now."

Marshall was shaking with nerves and anger. Alexander quickly scooted back to his seat, hands in the air. Marcos crawled out of the line of fire and stood up a few feet from the car.

The military man walked up alongside him, "I'm Charles Chenard and this is my partner, Marshall Dunnett. Are you okay?" Charles reached out a steadying hand for Marcos. "Put the gun down, Marshall. He gets your point." Marshall slowly lowered the gun but didn't take his finger off the trigger or his eyes off of Alexander. Charles looked back to Marcos with concern on his face.

Marcos pointed at Alexander and said, "He is one of them, one of those things. I…I saw it come out of the ground. It was humanlike, but then not, and all those teeth, and the black eyes." Charles shook Marcos gently on the shoulder and asked, "What are you talking about? Something back at the gas station? When you opened the rifts?"

"Rifts?" asked Marcos dazedly.

"That's what Alexander calls them. You say he is one of them. You mean Project Ostium?"

Marcos stared vacantly into the distance. "A monster. It was reptilian and manlike in shape. It came out of the ground where my car was. It all happened so fast. I was unable to move away from it so I closed my eyes to make it go away. When I opened them it was still there, cut in half. Then, all sorts of these holes, rifts as you said, opened everywhere. I couldn't stop it, the screams. God, I can still hear them all screaming as they fell into the rifts."

Charles held on to Marcos by his shoulders as he started to shake uncontrollably with fright. Charles had never seen anyone have such a breakdown; he had thought for a second it was a seizure the shaking was so violent. He started guiding the distraught Marcos towards the safe house. "Marshall, bring Alexander. We need to get off this street."

The safehouse smelled of stale food and old mold. The house had well-worn furniture and the sad remnants of cutlery left behind by the previous owner from decades ago. The fridge held food placed by the CIA for those needing its safety, but the quality was questionable and the quantity sparse. Charles threw together some barebones bologna sandwiches for everyone and then had Marcos sit down and tell them everything he could think of. Hours passed quickly as he told his story in detail and was forced to go over details again and again as Charles tried to poke holes in it to get as much truth as he could be sure was given. After midnight, Marcos found it impossible to continue and was helped to a couch in the living room by Charles. When Charles returned to the kitchen, he took a long deep breath. He was mentally drained from the information overload he had just extracted from Marcos.

"Well, that story nearly rivals yours, Alexander." Charles filled up a cup of coffee and sat down at the small kitchen table. The helicopters had long since gone quiet in their flyovers and an eerie calmness had settled outside. The house provided little comfort for Charles's nerves and he kept constantly looking outside the backdoor window.

Alexander kept stealing glances into the living room at Marcos. "He lies. There is no way some janitor has been blessed with the powers."

"Blessed!?" exclaimed Marshall, unable to sit. He was pacing the kitchen while cradling his cup of coffee in his hands. "I would hardly call being able to summon a demon, or whatever the hell that was blessed."

Alexander leaned his head back and stared at the ceiling, tired of Marshall's voice. "I have told you already; this is a gift. This is the gift they have talked about in the Project from the day I was brought in. Great power they said."

Charles asked, "They said this power specifically?"

"Well, no. I'd heard rumors of what Colonel McDaniel can do and he was able to do it by being elevated by The First. Details were always vague, but I have seen McDaniel do exactly what Marcos described." He paused for a second then continued, "I went there. Where all those people from the gas station have now gone." He shivered.

Charles noticed the shiver and hint of fear in Alexander's voice. "That scares you? That place?"

Alexander slowly brought his head back down from staring at the ceiling and locked eyes with Charles, "That thing he mentioned coming out of the rift. It is real and intelligent. Not the same as us, I suppose, but still intelligent. They are ancient and have one goal. To come here."

"So, they are aliens? Like in another dimension or something?" Marshall asked.

"No one ever discussed it," Alexander said, "No one had ever seen them beyond Colonel McDaniel, and anything about him or what he knew was nothing more than rumor or myth in the Project. I think they are of this world, but have left it or moved on somehow. But now they want to come back."

"Why don't they just come back, then? Why give someone like Marcos this power?" Marshall's voice held disbelief in it as he barraged Alexander his questions. Alexander's only reply was to spread his hands open and shrug his shoulders, a smirk crossing his face. Marshall leaned on the table and stared at Alexander, trying to persuade him to give more, but Alexander became silent and would not meet his gaze.

Charles, seeing the pointless standoff said, "Then that is our enemy. Otherworldly beings that are using individuals to open these 'rifts' to get back to our world. Yet, Marcos said that it dissolved shortly after entering our world and being cut in half by the rift closing. Something is wrong with them; they must be trapped. They must be finding another way." He pointed to Alexander's hand which had just started showing scales under the bluish skin. Alexander glanced down at his hand and quickly put it under the table.

Marshall straightened up and leaned far away from Alexander, "Oh, shit. That's it! You are becoming one of them." Alexander stiffened and turned white. Marshall pressed his point. "No words on that matter either I bet. Charles, we should get rid of him. If he's one of them then how much is he hiding. How do we know this isn't like that movie 'The Thing' and he is just some kind of doppelganger here to change us?" Marshall's hand gripped the pistol on his hip tightly.

"It's not like that! It's not something that is contagious, I swear!" Alexander was suddenly shouting.

Charles said, "I think, if it was like what you are suggesting Marshall, he would already have gotten us. We have all been asleep, easy targets for any attack from him. No, something else happened to him when he was sent into that rift by Ambassador McDaniel. Something he hasn't told us yet. Right?"

Alexander was shaking as he defended himself, "You don't know, you just can't fucking understand what was in there. I'm not with them! You think I want this! I'm dying!" He slammed his hands on the table and stood up. Marshall moved to stop him but Alexander brushed passed him as he started for the door to the backyard.

Charles gestured for Marshall to stop. The door slammed behind Alexander. "Let him be. He has nowhere to go."

Marshall said, "We can't trust him. He is hiding too much." Marshall moved towards the living room, leaned on the kitchen wall and gestured towards Marcos who remained sound asleep, "And him, do you think he told us the truth? A lowly janitor that just happened to get caught up in something as crazy as this."

Charles considered the sleeping figure as he slowly sipped his coffee. "He seemed very earnest in his story and never contradicted himself. Yes, I think he is being honest with us. The fear in his eyes is just too real and open. The real question is, what is really going on with him, and what can he actually do?"

"So, what's our next move? They don't expect us to stay here for long, do they?"

"No, but I think we will be wishing for just that soon enough. They will likely be shuffling us all over, to stay one step ahead of the military searching for Marcos. It's our job to figure out how we can use him to our advantage." Marshall gave him a sidelong stare and said, "Our advantage? We rescued him, so aren't they going to take him off our hands? Man, we can't get into this any deeper."

Charles gave a mock laugh, "Deeper? We are already six feet deep and everyone is going to start throwing dirt on us until we stop breathing. We've got to fight for ourselves from here on out.

Director Washington said that he had few to trust and that the connections to this Project Ostium run deep in the military and the FBI. We are alone and need to stay hidden as best we can until our next move."

"What kind of move are you thinking?"

Charles didn't answer Marshall. He finished his coffee and turned around to see Alexander coming back inside. Alexander had a defeated look on his face, "They talked to me."

Charles placed his cup down without ever letting his eyes leave Alexander for a moment. "Who talked to you?"

"When I was in that other world. The First talked to me. Well, they don't talk. It was just images in my head but I understood them perfectly. They showed me what is coming. How they are coming to our world."

Marshall said, "Why didn't you tell us that earlier? Seems like something we needed to know, don't ya think?"

"Because I didn't. They have me; I have no choice in that. This transformation is going to happen and I don't think I will be me anymore once it is done. They want me to sabotage as much as I can before I die."

Marshall had his hand back on his gun, "See, I told you he is one of them. A damn mole placed in with us! I should kill him right now!"

Charles shook his head at Marshall and said, "Slow down. We are not just shooting him. Alexander, are you in contact with them now? Can you feel what they are planning?"

Alexander said, "No, not quite. But every moment that passes I can feel a presence approaching. Like a wave far off coming into shore." He gestured towards Marshall and said, "I don't blame him for wanting to kill me, but know that I can help you stop them." Marshall started to speak but kept his words to himself. He saw the wheels turning inside Charles's head and grudgingly knew that without Alexander, any plan they came up with would be them flying blindly. He never took his hand off his pistol and he didn't like how much had changed so quickly, especially inside him. Paranoia was infesting his mind and he couldn't shake it and he knew he wouldn't shake it, not while Alexander remained with them.

Henry Almond saw the rift close above him as he slammed into soft ground. His last view was of a clear night sky and Marcos Romano's face staring wide eyed at him as the rift snapped shut instantly. The view was replaced by a pale white sky which was lit with an equally pale-yellow light that seemed to come from everywhere and yet nowhere. The screams of dozens of people surrounded him, along with car alarms blaring across the swamp-like landscape. He jumped to his feet, looked around, and felt his stomach fill with excitement at the sight he saw. Dozens of the reptilian creatures, such as the one that had come through at the gas station, were swarming over the others that had fallen through before him.

He searched for a direction that was clear of any cars or people. Finding an empty space among the chaos he started backing up from the carnage, never taking his eyes off the carnage before him. He knew he needed to stay far from the killing or else become a ravaged and dead part of it. The reptilians were walking on two legs, swishing long meaty tails behind them as they pounced on people. They were not simply killing. They were reveling in the violence. People were struggling against them as the beasts overpowered them, taking huge bites out of limbs and torsos. Some people had arms and legs ripped clean off their bodies. They staggered around in a daze as they screamed and cried. The sound of breaking glass and metal tearing filled the air just as much as the screams. The beasts were tearing people out of cars, viciously throwing them to the ground where they ripped them apart.

A huge reptilian with the remains of a small arm dangling from its gore-filled mouth looked at him and started approaching. Almond spread his arms wide to show neither resistance nor fear. The beast approached in long loping strides until it was only a few feet away. It towered over him. He guessed it must have been nearly eight feet tall, much larger than the others. Its pale blue skin was rippling with muscles, its arms thick and long with humanlike hands that ended in dagger shaped claws. He could feel its hot breath even at this distance and the copper smell of blood was thick and heavy on the air around it.

"I am a follower, a devout worshiper of The First," he said, slowly and loudly. He spoke one of the calls to worship he had been taught: "Hear the terror of the past. It is a rumble in the chests of those that believe. A tremor to ripple around the world. Commit now to the way it was, so it shall be again." The monstrous form before him went rigid and looked beyond him. Almond saw a primal fear in the eyes of the monster and turned to see what could have caused it.

At first, he saw nothing but endless white on an endless horizon only broken by skinny gnarled trees that appeared dead and rotting. He soon saw what the reptilian had seen-a shimmering form approaching in the distance. It began to rush towards him, sending a wind before it as it floated above the ground. Almond could see it was a pale white reptilian that was slender and tall, its clawed boney feet hovering above the ground. Its arms were outstretched toward him and a rush of images filled his mind. They were of a past long gone and dead. His mind was filled with destruction and chaos, fear entered his mind for the first time as the pale one imparted the emotion upon him.

"I see, yes. You are truly the most ancient and powerful of all." A sensation of his head being carved open with razor sharp claws cut off his words. He reflexively reached for the wound but found nothing. The pale reptile was now before him, still floating. Its white scaly skin spotted with dark scars all over its body caused by ancient fire that had nearly engulfed the Pale One long ago.

Almond was struck with blindness, the world disappearing to black, causing him to gasp in terror. When his vision started to return, he soon realized it was not his own. He was looking upon a small room, a kitchen. He could see two men in suits, they looked like agents of some kind and they both had guns on their hips. He was seeing through someone else's eyes. The view panned nauseatingly to the left and he saw a black-haired man sleeping on a couch in a darkened room. The sleeping man stirred and said something to the suits. Almond could see it was Marcos Romano. The vision went black again and he returned to his own eyes, staring at the Pale One again. The leader of The First.

"It was Marcos; you showed me him. I know I failed but I will not again. I will get him and show him his purpose, I promise." Pain lanced through his skull as a final vision formed. Another barrage of images entered his mind. They were of humanity being torn apart, the world rolling with destruction and change. The images were so real and so intense they caused him to lose his breath and fall to his knees in the soft mud. The large reptile standing behind him, that he had nearly forgotten about, placed its long-clawed fingers around his head and he felt a searing sensation as its hands became white hot against his skull. He screamed, felt the claw hands fall from his head, and a meaty crash of a collapsing body behind him. He looked back and saw the once great reptile was now nothing but a shriveled husk. Inside himself he felt something new, something hungry. "I have ascended!" he shouted to the sky.

The pale reptile closed its eyes. Minutes passed as Almond stared in awe at it, trying to figure out how a constant radiant shining light seemed to glow around it without any sign of its source. As he thought on the light a rift formed beneath him and, in an instant, he was slamming down hard on his knees upon the hard floor. The cold air of air conditioning made his body shiver. He looked up and saw Ambassador McDaniel standing before him; his hands finishing a movement as he closed the rift above him.

McDaniel looked with mocking eyes at Almond, "Looks like you have just been given a second life." Almond threw up on the floor as his head swam from all the knowledge it had been filled with. As he emptied his stomach, he heard McDaniel laughing at him, a hateful

laugh.

Project Ostium VII: Armageddon

Cretaceous Period: 65.5 million years ago
marshlands which will be known as Southern Missouri

The Pale One walked in great strides up the steep, forested hill. His muted white scales stretched tightly over his lean boney body as he used his long arms and clawed hands to grip young saplings to help himself up the hill. His reptilian face had a stubby round muzzle, small and less protruding compared to most of his kind, with rows of razor teeth and a long greyish tongue lancing out, tasting the air. Long, soft spines drooped in a row from the top of his head down to the tip of his tail. The spines were pale, blotchy, with black discoloration flaked throughout. Gaps in the vast coniferous forest canopy showed the deep blue sky above. A pair of giant winged reptiles, what will be known as pterosaurs, flew gracefully overhead, the beating of their leathery wings filling the quiet morning. The sun was just starting to peek over the top of the hill; its early morning rays beginning to heat the already warm land. He had no time for the majestic beauty of it all as his attention was fixated on a single point of light above him. Something large and bright had appeared in the sky a few days ago, growing bigger and closer with each passing day.

As he reached the top of the hill he looked back and saw only dense canopy over the marshland below that stretched far to the North and West. It was the warm swamp of his tribe; one small tribe among many that dotted the land, shrouded in a dense fog that often hung over it in the morning. He turned back to the bright light in the sky, now seeing it framed perfectly through the treetops. He closed his eyes to focus and block out the loud buzz of insects and the occasional stabbing pain in his long, agile feet from the reddish-brown needles that littered the forest floor.

As the Pale One stood alone he could feel all the members of his tribe in the back of his mind. A never-ending collection of images racing through his head, showing every sight and thought of his people. Through this collective connection they could even reach out to other tribes far to the North and a continent away to the South, through this they knew themselves as The First.

His mind, along with all the elders, had been flooded recently with images of the bright light in the sky from the tribes farther south. From the southern tribes' perspective, it appeared to be falling upon them. The elders of his people had ignored these images and concerns, seeing them as worries from far away. For the Pale One, a deep nauseating sickness filled his stomach each time he saw the images, and he found himself unable to dismiss them as casually as the elders had.

He had decided the previous night, a sleepless night, that he couldn't stand the sense of impending doom anymore. He had to act. At the first light of day, he'd sought out solitude to test himself. The First had many great powers and one of them was the ability to create other realities and open pathways from this world to those realities. They used these other realities to travel great distances, allowing them to escape and defend themselves from the many dangers of their world. Through this power, they had mastered the many predators that stalked the forests and swamps from the great Tyrannosaurus Rex, a two-legged beast with powerful jaws that towered over them, to the agile feathered killers, Deinonychus, that stalked the forests silently. These and many other threats had been mitigated as when the attack occurred a rift would be opened before the beast and send it into a reality created just for holding dangerous animals.

The greatest of The First, the elders, were the only ones allowed to wield this power of realities. They achieved it by focusing their minds and opening cuts or rifts into reality, allowing them to step through into a realm of their own creation to then be brought back out by someone in reality. It was a complex, and sometimes, fatal journey. Many had been lost in the other realities of creation and there had been failures to open the rift again that had led to those in the other realities to die upon returning to the world years later, if they ever returned at all. Because of these dangers, it was forbidden for anyone to attempt to open rifts into these realms or form other realities without the guidance of the elders. The Pale One understood the reason for the restrictions but knew he could not wait for the elders to help. He was on his own.

Under the morning light of the sun and the unnerving image of the bright light in the sky, the Pale One was ready to test not only his power of creation, but a new power that no one had ever tried before. Alone in the coniferous forest, warming beneath the hot sun's rays lancing through the treetops, he focused all his strength toward stopping the collective connection. Such a task was unheard of as it was the connection that gave them their knowledge, without it he would be isolated and alone.

As he concentrated on the connection, he imagined disassembling the threads that bound him to the others, one by one. He felt the elders of his tribe focus in on him, images of concern and distress filling their minds as they felt him slip away. They tried to reach out to him, to locate him, as they assumed, he was dying. He continued on; the images dimmed and flickered until they were no more.

The calm of not seeing through all the other's minds was terrifying at first. An emotion he had never truly experienced until that moment. As a collective, he could always rely on the reassurance of the others, and the help and safety of others knowing, if at any time, something was wrong. Without that connection, he was lost. Yet, he felt freedom.

A silence filled his very being. Through this silence he could imagine by himself, able to create alone at last. He opened a rift before him with a simple gesture of his long fingers. This rift was pitch black, currently unenterable as nothing existed beyond it. A rip in the fabric of the world awaiting him to begin. His mind raced to imagine, to create, the reality beyond, forming and molding it to what he wanted. He held an image of the marshlands that made his home, willing that image to fill the space beyond the rift he opened. The exertion was tremendous and he felt his head grow faint from the effort, yet the thrill of it kept him in the present. His long, boney tail swished in anticipation. He opened his eyes, dark green orbs with long pupil slits, and looked through the rift to the place that had formed beyond it. A perfect world stood beyond.

The Pale One stepped through the rift. It snapped away instantly as his strength to hold it open failed once in the imagined realm. He stood in his new land filled with lush, green trees and ankle-deep water. There was no sun in the sky. Only a pale, white light that emanated from everywhere and nowhere at once. Mud squished between his clawed toes as he curled them down into it, the smooth warmth comforting to him. He strode through the land, hope and joy filling his entire being. He had created a truly amazing place, a place to save his people.

When he was satisfied with his creation, he reconnected the mental link to the collective and was shocked to find an entire day had passed. The reconnection was staggering as a flood of images hit him, many desperate as those of his tribe had been searching for him from the very moment, he had severed the link. The images were of others imagining finding his dead body, a good guess as this was the only reason normally for a connection loss. The pain and fear of his loss on hundreds of his tribe was made vividly clear to him. He experienced guilt at how much he had enjoyed being alone and separate from all who cared for him. As the elders reached his mind, he felt their acknowledgment and mistrust. It only took a few seconds for them to realize what he had done. Swiftly, a rift was opened to the world by the elders and as he stepped through his clawed feet splashed down into the swamp waters of his home.

The air was stifling in the swamp as the sun reached its zenith in the sky, but went unnoticed among The First. The broad-leaf trees and dense ferns provided a nearly impenetrable cover from the hot sun. The Pale One knelt on his knees upon the moist, mossy ground of a small island in the swamp. He was surrounded by the four elders of his tribe. They were all bent over with crooked backs from age, their rough scales covered in moss from a sedentary life. They probed his mind for all he had seen and done while gone, struggling to figure out how he had cut the connection and just what he had done once it was cut. He blocked this effort by forcing them to continuously see his last image of the bright light in the sky and all the feelings of unease it was causing him. They cared not for his concerns and continued to scratch at his mind, tearing away at the image as best they could to see beyond it. He held out for hours but eventually images of the new reality he had created poured through. They hissed in unison to show their displeasure.

He tried again to change their minds, sending images of all The First traveling into his creation, safe, while elders stayed behind to provide a link back to the real world once the bright light and the doom it may bring had passed. He knew this was a possible death sentence for those elders but it weighed against the death of everyone else. The argument flowed back and forth. A silent argument that was only visually observable by the elders hissing and pointing at him, but the images that flowed between the elders and the Pale One were fast and aggressive. Others of the tribe could see the images as they raced across the collective but all did their best to ignore the scene despite the interest that was palpable over the images the Pale One showed of his new reality. Several young hatchlings ran around, near the island, playing a game of seeing who was brave enough to get close and try to touch the moss-covered scales of an elder.

The argument came to a sudden stop as a deafening thunder clap broke through the air. The sky was clear blue without a thunderstorm in sight yet it was unmistakable that the explosion came from above. The images that flooded their minds came from the southern tribe who were thousands of miles away across the southern sea. They were in a dire panic as the bright light was now a mountain sized raging fire falling from the sky towards them at incredible speed. A windstorm pressed down on those of the southern tribe, knocking all to the ground and leveling trees. The Pale One gasped and fell to the ground from the flood of emotions. The elders managed to keep their feet but were wavering under the mental assault.

The Pale One finally managed to stand and took off running for the hill that he had previously climbed to try and gain a view of the sky. They could all see the flaming light through the swamp canopy but as the Pale One, and several other tribesmen that had raced after him, started ascending the hill they could see clearly a great mountain of fire descending from the sky. The sight caused many to become paralyzed with fear and fall to the ground in terror. The Pale One was transfixed on the fiery mountain. He knew he didn't have much time by the speed at which it was falling.

They were on a steep angle halfway up the hill, but there was no time to get to the top or head back down. He waved his hand and opened the rift to his creation. He had no way of directly reaching the southern tribes, only a rift opened by one of the elders could create a path to his location. The elder realities could act as doorways between two points to allow travel over immense distances to occur near instantly. The biggest limitation to this form of travel was rifts could only be made so big, leading to only three or four abreast being able to pass through at once. He sent out a desperate image to the elders of the southern tribes, they responded by showing they had already begun. His own elders, finally having snapped out of their doubts, had breathlessly climbed up behind the Pale One, opening the rift for the southern refugees to pass through. The Pale One stretched out his pale arm and the rift to his creation opened as wide as he could make it. His tribesmen raced past him into his rift without question, they had all been given the images of the southern tribe by him. A mad scramble had begun up the hill as his tribe streamed by him. The once bright light in the sky that had turned into a fiery mountain descended swiftly over the horizon to the south.

The last image he received from the South was one of pure red flames. He saw the great mountain fall upon land and water of the southern lands, instantly blinding everything with a flash of light. All went silent for a moment and the last few survivors of the southern tribe came pouring through the elders' rift. These last few desperate creatures were engulfed in flames. They came tumbling out of the rift screeching in pain and falling to the ruddy brown ground of the hillside; rolling down the hill spreading flames among the dry needles. The elders closed the rift and started opening other ones for those still down in the swamp and to other tribes hundreds and thousands of miles to the north. There was chaos all around the Pale One as hundreds poured through four rifts onto the cramped hillside, staggering into his gateway. As the chaotic scramble through the rifts continued the land started to shake and vibrate. A tremendous earthquake was starting to overtake all the world. The trees swayed violently, casting long shadows as they shook. Loud tearing sounds filled the forest as the trees started ripping clear of their roots, toppling down with thunderous force.

The Pale One struggled to keep his footing as the earth shook but fell backwards, sliding down the hill as the earthquake continued. The ground beneath him was loose and sliding along with him down the hill. As he stared up, he saw the sky had become filled with black rock and fire rising high into the blue sky, a sky that was becoming redder and darker as it became choked with ash and fire. The earthquake abated but soon a great roaring filled the air, and as the Pale One slowly got to his feet, a deafening blast of wind whipped all around them from the south. The wind was made of hot ash swirling in torrents from the top of the sky to the ground. The Pale One could feel his skin burning and blistering as the temperature quickly rose. The very air he breathed was choking him from the ash and heat. He stumbled blindly up the hill towards the rift, all his senses muted by the rushing ash. He narrowly missed instant death as a great chunk of glowing hot rock crashed down to his left, exploding on impact and spraying up dirt and debris. He struggled to squint in the ashy air as his eyes were drying out. Explosions were occurring all around him as large rocks falling from the sky crashed down in great plumes of black ash and fire.

He was in such intense pain and agony he wanted to fall over and die to end it. His willpower was nearly spent when he tripped over a curled-up hatchling, a particularly small one whose body radiated with smoke and it's skin sizzled as it burned from the heat. He stuck out his arms as he fell and burned the palms of his hands on the searing ground. He pushed himself back up and started his slow, painful march towards where he hoped the rift was. The tiny hatchling latched on to the Pale One's leg, desperately digging its sharp claws into his leg with its last bits of strength. The Pale One did not pause for a second as he forced his way through the heat, now so hot he could smell his flesh burning. As he pushed through the blinding ash and heat, he found himself suddenly falling through his rift before he even realized he had reached it. The hatchling clung on tight as they tumbled through the rift. As they collapsed into the soothing waters of his creation, his strength gave out and the rift snap shut behind him. His power was greater than even he had known. Not even the greatest elder would have been expected to keep a rift open through all that trauma, but he had.

He had not realized how deafening the wind had truly been until it was gone. He found himself lying face down in the warm waters of his creation in near silence. He pushed himself up from the ground and reached down to pick up the burned hatchling that lay curled up at his feet, its fragile head bobbing slightly in the water. He picked it up and held it tight to his chest. It was weak but still breathing, its small eyes stared up at him tired and frightened. the Pale One's entire body screamed out in pain from the burns he had sustained, and as he looked around at all the others near him, he saw many others that had suffered the same fate as him. A lucky few that had stumbled through the rift after the ash wind had engulfed them. He reached out to the elders but felt nothing. They were all gone, having stayed behind to keep each rift open as long as they could.

He reached out to the connection of the collective for any others still alive in the real world. The few he reached disappeared from the connection as quickly as he found them. Images of fire and ash, of great waves of water from the ocean towering to the sky and rushing across the land, and of boiling heat that baked all in their skin were just some of the horrifying images he received. The world was lost to them, he was sure of that. He looked out at all of his people he had saved and saw it to be several thousand, but that was a small number compared to the untold tens of thousands of The First that had been alive earlier that day. He let out a tearing roar from the pain and for all those lost. Above all else he felt sadness for all those trapped with him. Without someone to open the rift on the other side they could not leave. For them, this was now a prison. No one aged in the other realms, all was static. Now, only madness and endless time awaited them.

Marcos screamed out in pain as his skin felt as if it were suddenly lit on fire and his mind raced with hundreds of images that he could not process. Charles and Marshall, who had been standing next to Marcos in the empty farm field, startled by his sudden outburst. They had been watching him test out, and learn to control his powers of opening rifts in the empty field strewn with bits of cornstalks and brown leaves. After briefly recovering from the shock of Marcos's scream, they rushed to his side to hold him up as he crumbled.

Charles reached him first, "Easy, easy, what just happened?" Marcos felt himself fainting but fought against it. He looked around as if he expected to see some unknown horror.

"I…I was suddenly filled with images or memories. And my skin was on fire, just as his skin was."

"Whose skin?" asked Charles.

Marcos looked at Charles with panic in his eyes, "One of those reptile men, like the one that came out of that rift at the gas station, only this one was pale white. He was some other place that wasn't the present. His memories, they were of the world ending."

Marshall had reached him now and was helping hold him steady, "You saw the world end? You mean in the future?"

"No, this must've been from when those reptilians were on earth. It was all swamps and dinosaurs. It must have been the time of the dinosaurs dying when that asteroid hit the earth. The reptilian monsters didn't know what it was but escaped through a rift."

Marcos slowly regained his grasp on the present, gingerly rising back to his feet. He shrugged off Charles and Marshall's helping hands and stared out across the barren field. The winter winds whipped the three men and cooled Marcos down from his phantom burns. He slowed his mind down and found he was able to piece through the previous onslaught of images more thoroughly.

Marshall said sternly, "We can't trust anything sent by those things. Sounds like they are trying to build sympathy or scare you." Marcos nodded in agreement, "I think you are right about the sympathy. But those images were real, I'm sure of that."

Marcos shivered violently in the cold breeze, the phantom burns having left him and heightened the sensation of the wind. "One thing the pale reptilian showed me was how he created the place the rift goes to. He created some kind of new world outside of time and space. That is how they are still alive. But, even still, the length of time they have spent there must have driven them mad. There are thousands of them, all crazed."

Charles said, "Well, if there are only thousands then at least we outnumber them with our billions."

Marcos shook his head, "They don't need their numbers. They just need people like me and like that Colonel McDaniel.

People they can manipulate and use to fight the battle for them. This is their world and they want to come back, but not with us here.”

Charles added, “Did you learn why you can do these things? Did they give you this power?”

Marcos shook his head in exacerbation with the barrage of questions, “I don't think so. I'm not sure it matters.”

“Of course, it does!” Marshall suddenly shouted at them, “If we are to fight this, we have to know how you and others like you can do this.”

Marcos turned on him, “Fight them how?! All I can do is open these rifts to their world, all I can do is help them with these powers. Everything just leads back to where they are, to help them escape.” He paused, staring out on the empty field again, “Best I just die; anyone with this power should just die. Then, at least, they would continue to be trapped.” He started walking back towards the farm house they were currently using as a safe house. The last several days they had hidden out at this farm to avoid all the military pressure on the nearby towns as the search for them continued.

Charles and Marshall let Marcos walk back alone. Charles waited until he was sure he was out of earshot before he spoke, "We can't let him fall apart. He is the only link to all this crazy shit and the only person with these powers we know is on our side."

Marshall spat into the cornfield. He could taste the hot moist air from the rifts being opened by Marcos's training at the back of his throat, "But how? He has a point. All we are doing is opening these pathways to the very place we don't want anyone to go, or anything to come from. What possible use could that be?" Charles had no answer. He walked back towards the house, his mind drawn to one part of Marshall's story in particular; the reptilians could create worlds, which may mean Marcos can create worlds. He mulled over how this could be used to their advantage as he reached the small one-story house with weathered siding and rotting roof tiles.

Charles and Marshall found Marcos shoving his clothes into the green duffel bag they had picked up at a previous safe-house. Charles asked, "Where do you think you're going? I can't let you just leave."

Marcos zipped the bag in one violent motion then lugged it over his shoulder. "Look, you guys don't have a clue what to do. We have been running around hiding from the army for days, and I am tired of it. I have parents that have not heard from me in weeks. I have to check on them."

Marshall slammed his fist against the wall. "Do you think we are just hanging out here for fucking fun!? Do you think we don't have families? We're doing all this to try and find a way to stop whatever is happening."

Marcos yelled back, "What? What is it that we have figured out? We don't have a clue about how to fight this, and barely know what we are fighting." Silence fell between them as Marshall struggled to think of something to counter with but couldn't think of anything. He knew he felt the same hopelessness as Marcos. Marcos stalked past him and into the living room where a bundle of blankets on the couch hid the form of Alexander. The pale blue light in the dimly lit room shone on his face, peeking out of the top of the blankets as he sat hunched forward staring into the television.

Alexander was changing, faster than anyone wanted. His skin had become covered in bluish scales and his hands and feet had started to grow long and clawed. He was slowly becoming one of The First. A tragic consequence of failing to stop Charles and Marshall and being brought before The First. His shiny scaly head glittered in the television's constantly flickering light.

Alexander spoke, his voice hoarse as the changes slowly took his ability to speak, "It is everywhere." Marcos stopped in his tracks and looked down at Alexander. He had avoided him as much as he could over the last several days. Alexander was a terrifying reality of the monsters they face. A reminder that Marcos actively avoided looking at. Marcos looked to the television and saw scenes of what he had done splashed across it. The reporter was stark white and obviously confused as she tried to explain what security camera footage was showing of great black holes opening up and swallowing people and cars. He dropped his bag and started shaking as he saw it wasn't him the security camera was showing. *"No explanation has been given yet for the multiple sightings of strange openings that have started to appear throughout the country. The number of victims from these could be in the thousands as reports of missing people continue to flood in. This morning, the President held a press conference on the White House lawn declaring a national emergency and, due to the still unknown source of the threat, a declaration of Martial Law. The National Guard and Army Reserves are being deployed to support local law enforcement…"* The television and lights in the house went out plunging the room into darkness. Everyone froze in place as their eyes adjusted to the dark that was compounded by the curtains being drawn, letting only a faint reddish light from the outside.

"Damn, do you think they cut the power?" exclaimed Marshall.

Charles responded, "Probably had a person like Marcos at the power plant. Everything is going crazy out there I'm sure."

Alexander spoke in his hoarse voice, now filled with pain, "My God, I can feel them. Images are flooding my mind. Stop! It's too much!" He screamed the last words and bent forward with long clawed fingers clutching his head, the fingers barely recognizable as human.

Charles had passed Marshall and stood beside Marcos, both staring down at Alexander in concern. Charles asked, "Do you see more images?" Marcos shook his head no.

Alexander brought his hands down so quickly the long claws cut shallow wounds down the sides of his bald head. He looked up at them, his face a contortion of pain as he spoke, "The Pale One is calling out to all of us that are changed or changing. He needs us to gather at a place far from here. The base, the military base Marcos spoke of. He is calling for us to gather." He viciously whipped his head around as if he could shake the images from his mind. "He needs us to be united. That is his plan, to have those like me, the ascended, unite on this end to help focus his power." He looked away and cradled his head again, whispering the word "stop" over and over again.

Marcos said, "It makes sense. He needs to form a large collective on this side. The abilities are some kind of psychic power that relies on a collection of users to make it powerful."

Marshall asked, "Yet, not you. Why didn't you get the message?"

Marcos replied, uncertainly, "Perhaps it does not work across species that well. Or he needs to trust those that are going to help him and that is why they are changing people." He looked around in the dark room between Marshall and Charles's faces as he spoke, "I know the images that were shown to me are real. These things did face a terrible fate, but they are changed, crazed after all this time. I can feel the sickness of insanity in them. They can't even reach out to us without hurting us like they are doing to Alexander." He paused and looked down at the duffle bag, a dark lump on the faded carpet. "I know there is no running from this. I still don't see how to stop it." He felt the hopelessness of the situation overwhelm him. His head swam nauseatingly as he tried to make himself realize he was going back to that base, back to the scratching in his skull.

Charles opened the curtains letting in the bright light of the sun upon the dingy room. "Alexander, lead us directly to the meeting. I will contact Director Washington and hopefully he can help us get in or even provide support. With Marcos, we can fight our way in if necessary and shutdown the source of all of this."

Marcos was still blinking against the harsh light. "But how do we know it is even possible or that such a chance will show up?"

Charles responded calmly and with a leveled voice, "We don't know for sure. But we do know everything is going to continue to fall apart and get worse the longer we stand around here doing nothing. We have one option left, and that is to act on this moment. It will not come again."

They bundled up Alexander, hiding his disfigured body the best they could and took off from the farm. The two-lane state highway was eerily empty and the fear of unknown military checkpoints started to weigh heavily on all of them. They would have to take country roads and avoid all major cities. Each stop they made in a small-town gas station showed them more news of a country in chaos. Power was intermittently going on and off throughout the country, entire cities were being quarantined by the military for reasons no one knew. Rumors of invasion from another country or even extraterrestrial in nature were being spouted off everywhere they went. Alexander had told them every branch of government had members that were a part of Project Ostium, and it was flexing that power by locking down the entire country, dividing and confusing any resistance that could form.

Project Ostium VIII: Into the Void

The winter-bare forests of the Ozark Mountains stood in silent contrast to the vibrant tropical landscape that was burned into Marcos Romano's mind. He found himself struggling to stay in the present as the foreign, ancient memories grew in strength with every mile that passed. A mental connection with The First had been made, distant and not fully formed but a connection nonetheless. He kept his eyes focused on the cold forest to ground himself in his reality, the real reality. His left arm was cradled in his lap with a thick bandage of gauze wrapped over blood-soaked cotton balls. The pain helped him stay grounded, and for that small grace, he was thankful.

Alexander let out a low sound that vibrated from deep inside his nasal cavity. To Marcos the sound reminded him of a slow air leak on a balloon that kept getting plugged causing a rhythmic trill to develop. The sound was alien in nature and caused the hair to stand up on the back of his neck. Marcos was doing everything he could not to look across the backseat at Alexander. He tried to focus on the trees again but the pain in his arm and the images of a long dead past would not leave.

The attack by Alexander on Marcos had been swift and without warning. It occurred as they made their way down a back-country road in Illinois. They were all tired and worn out from the endless hours of driving. Marcos had looked over and noticed Alexander had folded over in his seat. They had dressed him in a grey hoodie that covered his rapidly changing form, but Marcos could see that the wide split mouth and rows of razor teeth that lined it had started to protrude out forming a short muzzle with long roping spit flickering out from haggard breaths. Marcos had leaned toward Alexander with his arm outstretched when the attack came. He saw the mouth stretching impossibly wide as it lunged toward his arm, sinking dozens of teeth into it. His scream made Marshall, who was driving at the time, jump in his seat and slam the brakes, bringing the car to a jolting stop.

After the attack, Alexander had quickly retreated back against his seat right after he had bitten Marcos's arm; acting just as confused and scared as Marcos felt about it. His reptilian face hiding emotion, only his blue, human eyes showed fear and regret. The last remnants of the man that was barely holding on inside. Charles had quickly administered first aid to Marcos's arm while Marshall hastily tied up Alexander's arms with his own shoe laces. His shoes having long since been removed as they no longer fit his widening feet and sharpening toenails.

Marcos leaned forward in his seat, careful not to brush his throbbing arm against anything while avoiding looking at Alexander in his periphery, and said to Charles who was now driving, "We're close now. I can feel them."

Charles and Marshall gave each other wearied looks. They had reached their limits with Alexander's insane transformation and Marcos's increasingly cryptic words. Charles replied, "I'm going to need a heads-up before we stumble directly upon the entrance to this base. We've made it this far without trouble; don't need to push that luck by running right into the very people we are avoiding."

Marshall jabbed a thumb at the hunched figure of Alexander, "I thought he was supposed to be guiding us?"

"Does he look like he can help us much anymore?!" Charles shouted with exacerbation and fatigue.

"That's my point!" Marshall lashed back. "This is all unraveling out of our control. We need to turn around and get back in touch with Director Washington. There is no way he wants us to take this on by ourselves."

Charles shook his head and said, "You know I have tried to contact him. Have I not called constantly? He is gone as far as we are concerned. No, we do this now."

The long drive had hit home how quickly the world was falling apart for Marcos. The military had imposed Martial law on the country, which had made the roads nearly empty and anytime they came close to an interstate they would see convoys of troops and tanks rolling down them. Occasionally the nighttime horizon would be lit with a deep red showing great fires in the distance and when the sun came up the smoke plumes that dotted the horizon in all directions confirmed the level of devastation that was occurring. What was the cause and how it was happening remained a mystery that they had speculated on little. The possible answers too horrible and out of their control to contemplate. The radio had gone dark, only giving off emergency signals or static on all channels.

"The base is close," said Marcos, "I didn't drive to work from this direction, but I believe we have a couple curves then when it starts to go downhill. The turn should be on our right. It's just a gravel road with a single guard post at the front." He heard it now. *The scratching, oh God, it had returned.* It raked at his skull as it had before, alien and uncaring in its sensations.

As they made the last curve before the road started to dip out of the hills and down toward a valley Alexander became violently animated. He threw back his hood with long bluish clawed hands, fully revealing the scaly skull underneath. His pupils had started to elongate into snake eyes, the blue fading to an emerald green. His wide mouth hung open with a dark, red tongue hanging out, tasting the air. He let out a long hiss that reverberated into his chest and started banging against the door.

"Stop! Stop!" shouted Charles as the car vibrated from the powerful blows against the door by Alexander. He pulled over to the gravely shoulder, the tires slipping in the cold mud and rocks as it came to a stop. The door gave under a final, powerful, full-body slam, and Alexander went sprawling out the door. As his body twisted out of the car, his long, thick tail lashed out towards Marcos who cracked his head against the window as he moved to avoid it slashing his face. Cold, biting air filled the car as the three remaining passengers stared in horror at Alexander as he stood to his full height.

Alexander had been a large man but the transformation only added to his considerable height. Hunched over in the car for hours the others had been unable to fully appreciate the extreme amount of changes that had been occurring to Alexander. The grey hoodie was stretched around his form and dark faded blue jeans ripped at the seams under the strain of his legs' increased size. The monstrous reptilian that stood outside the car looked back at them with black slit pupils. The red tongue shot out at them through the pale blue lips, showing a hint of blood-stained teeth inside.

Marcos felt completely exposed as the reptilian head looked back at him through the gaping hole where the door had been. He prepared his mind to open a rift if Alexander should charge, but he looked away and started stalking off into the forest in long loping strides. Marcos let out a great sigh realizing he had been holding his breath as he had tensed up for the attack.

Charles's eyes, along with everyone else's, were fixated on the spot in the forest where Alexander had disappeared into. "Well, I guess this is what I wanted. Let's go after him." He pulled the slide back on his Walther pistol to double check a round was already inside. Satisfied he opened his door and started after Alexander. He heard two car doors slam behind him and heard the ungraceful footfalls of Marshall and Marcos follow after. He felt adrenaline racing through him, his heart beating in his chest. He hated marching off into the unknown, dragging Marshall along to a possibly certain death, but he knew there were no options left for anyone. The country was in flames from this threat, and this was likely the only chance to stop it.

Keeping pace with Alexander proved impossible. His long strides placed him far out of view most of the time, but he appeared to Charles to be going in nearly a straight line. They dipped down to a shallow creek and back up a steep hill to emerge in an open field filled with thigh high brown grass. Marshall and Marcos were breathing heavily behind him as they caught up to him at the edge of the field. Charles had just made out a faint image of Alexander disappearing across the field and around a jutting bit of forest that stretched out into the field.

"Jesus, he is fast," wheezed Marshall, massaging a stitch in his side. Charles motioned them on across the field. He could clearly see the path Alexander had made in the grass and a gut feeling told him they were close. Marcos confirmed this, "I can't explain why but I believe the base is just around the corner of that tree line. It is only a couple nondescript grey concrete buildings, no flags or major parking lot to give it away. Everything is underground."

Charles said with genuine concern, "How are you doing? We need you to be able to fight with us when we get there." Marcos did not seem to register he had even spoken, but before Charles could ask his question again Marcos nodded his acknowledgement and took off through the field.

Marshall was more reluctant. He hung back as they marched across the field. His gun was held tightly in his sweaty palm as he whipped his head around expecting to see soldiers or even other reptilian monsters to come storming across the field at them. Charles wanted to calm him but found he had no words for it. He felt the same fear and knew each one of them just had to deal with it himself.

A series of long one-story grey buildings stood in the distance just as Marcos had predicted. They were overgrown with vines and had years of dirt and mud caked on the outside. They appeared abandoned, just as the military wanted them to look. They saw Alexander moving around the side of the structure and disappear from sight.

Marshall's breath was puffing out in great misting breaths in the cold air as he struggled to catch his breath. He said breathlessly, "I figured they would be meeting outside. Are we going inside that building?" A quivering of fear was in his voice.

Charles tried to think of other options but could not come up with any. The plan had never really been much of a plan; follow Alexander, hope that the leaders of this were present, and take them out as fast as he could. Marshall continued to speak, giving voice to his fears, "How do we know this isn't just a trap for us? They know we have Marcos, and they probably know about Alexander." Charles had no argument to give but simply nodded and started off towards the grey buildings.

Marcos and Marshall traded uneasy looks, fear stark in their eyes, and hurried after Charles. The sense of unease and being exposed in the open field hurried their steps. Charles waited for them at the corner of the building, and then the three of them, single file, went around the corner and saw two more similarly abandoned looking concrete structures with a simple circle drive linking them together. No flag or signs to announce what the buildings were or held within. There were no vehicles to be seen. Marcos pointed to an underground entrance to the parking garage situated just off of the farthest building from them. "That leads down to the only access points to the buildings that I know of."

They descended into the garage. The guard post at the entrance stood abandoned with a radio beeping slowly inside of the small glass hut. They made their way through the first lot that was filled with cars.

"Where is everyone?" muttered Marcos.

"Not around here, thankfully," replied Marshall who had regained his breath but kept his voice low in case he turned out wrong. His hands were sweating so profusely the gun threatened to slip right out of his hand. He moved in an amateur imitation of Charles, both hands on his pistol, checking side to side as they made their way through the garage. Charles did not mind, hoping Marshall's focus on trying to act like him would calm him.

They continued deeper into the base, unease building as they passed by empty security checkpoints. The path into the depths of the base was wide open, guiding them deep into the bowels of the installation. No sound could be heard as they descended stairwells and walked long hallways, guided by Marcos. The eerie silence was broken by the sound of barking orders coming from the lowest floor of the base. Marcos had them pause at the top of the last stairwell that led down to a single, large metal door.

"This is it, "Marcos said, "Through that door is a long hallway with no doors off the side of it, only the final door at the end. Beyond that, I have no idea where it goes."

Charles knew it was a trap. Anyone could see that. The sound of voices filled the space beyond the door below them, but they seemed to be fading away. "How are you holding up Marcos?" Charles saw beads of sweat pouring down the man's face.

"It hurts," Marcos wiped the sweat from his brow on his soaked coat sleeve. "It's all so close here. The First must be at the end of the hallway. It's down there that I first felt them, their scratching in my skull." He grew quiet and stared down the steps to the windowless door. The voices on the other side had gone quiet, but he could feel a static charge in the air as something else grew louder.

Marcos's eyes lit up with panic. "I hear a voice, a young voice. Almost like a whisper." He started descending the stairs with his head oddly cocked up listening to the phantom voice. Charles followed after him with Marshall, who was far more hesitant about approaching the door, a few steps behind them.

"I thought they only communicated through images?" asked Charles.

"No, this is not them. Definitely human. They must have a child. Maybe someone like me."

Charles reached out and stopped Marcos's hand as it reached for the long door handle. "Wait, let me go first. Be ready with your ability in case someone with a gun is at the far end of this hallway."

Marcos let go but stood directly behind Charles as he pulled on the door handle and pushed in. A breeze hit them as the door swung open, the air hot and moist as it always is when it pours out of the rifts. The hallway was bright white from fluorescent lights. Despite this, all the light terminated at the far end where blackness gaped back at them through a rectangular door frame. Voices could be heard again but only faintly.

Charles had his pistol raised as he led the way down the hallway towards the void before them. Shadows flickered in the darkness beyond showing the movement of dozens of individuals. Charles quietly mouthed back over his shoulder to Marcos, "Is that some kind of rift?"

Marcos barely heard Charles's words over the child's voice that filled his head. "Yes, a massive one, held open by what must be a supreme effort. Must be the doing of the First. I can only imagine how powerful and skilled they have become over the millions of years that have passed."

Marshall had stopped following them halfway down the hallway. He called out in a wobbly voice filled with emotion, "Guys, stop! I can't go in there."

Charles stopped but never took his eyes off the black void before him. He hissed at Marshall, "Keep your voice down, damn it. We can't split up. We're all going in there together." Charles gave a quick glance behind him. Marcos was pressed against his back, which is exactly where Charles wanted him. Marshall was taking shuffling footsteps backwards from them. Charles started to speak to Marshall but froze as he saw the entrance door opening and a large man that was in the process of changing into one of the First emerged from it. He could not bring his gun around to shoot as Marshall blocked any clear shot he would have.

"Marshall! Behind you!" Charles saw the half-formed reptilian monster rush towards Marshall with bounding feet. Marcos suddenly started yelling right in his ear and he turned around to see that out of the void doorway, which had only been about five feet away when they stopped, stood a figure. An army officer in all black fatigues and black beret stood with a pistol pointed at them. The officer appeared hardly more visible than the shadows dancing in the void behind him as his black fatigues and dark skin blended in as if he were a natural part of the void.

Charles looked into the dark brown eyes of the officer and could see the cold killer behind them. The man could kill him at any moment and Charles knew it. Marshall let out a terrified scream, and Charles turned around and started running towards him, knowing the officer could shoot him at any moment. Marcos had fallen back against the stark white walls and appeared paralyzed at the sight of the beast that had picked up Marshall by his throat and was stalking towards them.

Charles and the beast were in a head-on collision. He brought his gun up as he ran and fired, hitting the left arm of the beast. Another gun went off and Charles felt pain lance through his right shoulder as he tumbled to the ground just as the beast carrying Marshall reached him. Its large, half-transformed feet stepped on his head and back, driving him down into the concrete ground. He lay prone on the floor as he heard the beast say in a deep voice, "See the glory of it, Marcos. See what they have done for me. No longer Henry Almond but something greater. They have won, and you are going to help finish it." Marcos yelled something incoherent but was soon muffled. A short time later, Charles knew he was alone in the hallway.

He slowly got to his feet. The pain in his shoulder screamed through him, and he swayed dangerously. His vision was blinded by the fluorescent lights, leaving his vision blurry as he peered down the hall. He leaned against the wall for a moment until his vision started to clear and looked at his shoulder. The bullet had gone straight through and he was unable to move his arm without his vision growing dark from the pain. He reached down with his left hand and retrieved his gun. The door to the void stood open without any sign of the officer, the beast, or the others. The shadows that had been moving in it were gone too, only an inky blackness remained. He walked into the void. The blood that flowed from his wound turned cold on his arm as it dripped off the end of his numbing fingertips.

Project Ostium IX: A Desperate Gambit

Marcos Romano refused to give up. Marshall laid unconscious and limp in the scaly arms of the beast that used to be Henry Almond, his former neighbor and apparent government spy. The man that had shot Charles, possibly even killed, followed as a dark cloud behind them. He had given his name as Colonel Nathan McDaniel of the U.S. Army, and promised he would kill Marcos if he tried to run as he waved him on with his pistol.

Marcos looked around the bleak landscape, desperate to see some way out. He remembered the images of this place sent to him by the ancient reptilian known as the Pale One. Its memories were from millions of years ago. Among the memories of that ancient world that was engulfed in fire and death he had seen the Pale One create the place he currently wandered through. As he looked around, he noticed the place he had been shown and the place he now saw stood in stark contrast from each other. The images given to him had been of lush plant life and dense swampland. What lay around him was more a decaying pile of rotted wood in an endless, shallow sea of mud.

"What has happened to this place?" Marcos said softly, not wanting his voice to carry too far in the emptiness. Colonial McDaniel replied, "What do you mean by that?" His tone was confused and inquiring, but with an edge of menace that threatened violence from any answer he deemed poor.

Marcos jumped slightly at the closeness of Daniel's words. *He must be walking right behind me, ready to kill me at any moment.* He furtively looked over his shoulder at the tall, imposing figure of McDaniel. He saw the gun gripped firmly in the man's hand. He knew there was no point in trying to lie. This was a man that would likely kill him no matter what he said. So he answered, "I mean, I have seen what this place looked like when it was first created. It was lush and bright. But now, it is decaying and darkening." It was darkening. The place he had seen in the ancient image had been bright as day, but this world hung in a pale dusk.

McDaniel walked up alongside Marcos, his gun casually swinging in his hand at his side. Marcos looked up at him then looked away quickly after seeing the simmering rage that danced in McDaniel's eyes. McDaniel seemed to contemplate Marcos's words for a few moments before replying, "They are dying, and the land with them. It's a testament to their great powers that they have lasted this long." Marcos could hear contempt and disdain in McDaniel's voice despite the positive words he spoke of the First. Perhaps McDaniel was not a devout follower like Almond. Marcos looked down at the misty, wet ground that squished beneath his shoes, soaking his socks with silty mud, and said, "Is that why you are helping them? Their power?"

McDaniel shot a glance at the scaly back of the Almond beast carrying Marshall, then in a low, calm voice answered, "You think the power you have touched is what they have? That is only a small taste of what the Pale One is capable of. I was the first man they encountered, and the great Pale One showed me all that he can do. He awoke the power in me and, with it, I single handedly took over the entire military base here."

Marcos said, "The reward must have been great. Did you kill your own men? How many are dying right now back in the real world?" Marcos couldn't believe the recklessness of his words but they continued to spill from him. "The country was falling apart as we drove to get here, cities burning. I can't see what would make all that worth it." As he said the words he looked right at McDaniel. He searched the dark brown eyes for any sign of emotion or care. He saw only a slight twitch form at the corner of one eye as he mentioned the killing of his men.

McDaniel's response was cool and measured. "I can see you feel you have the moral high ground. You care not for my story unless it furthers your belief that I am evil and have done everything I have done for selfish reasons. But know that life is not good versus evil. It is grey." He pointed his gun towards the reptilian figure of Almond striding several paces ahead of them. "They are trying to survive. But to do it they need us gone. I didn't do anything for some great reward. I'm not their worshipper or lapdog. They cannot be defeated easily because we cannot easily reach them. This is their creation and they control much of what occurs here, but not all." He looked at Marcos, his head tilted down since he stood nearly a foot taller and continued, "I am a survivor. And that means playing along until exactly the right moment. Now that you are here the moment is close."

The reptilian beast that was Henry Almond stopped and turned back towards them, its round, distended snout showed rows of razor-sharp teeth as it grinned menacingly at them and hissed, "We are close now. You will soon be shown your greatness, Marcos. You

are to Ascend higher than all the rest." His words were garbled as he

struggled to form them in his mutated mouth. Almond continued

speaking but quieter, as if reminding himself. "I have achieved the

great reward myself but so much more still awaits me." A wild,

beastly look filled his eyes. Marcos could still hear the words of the

human it had once been, but the eyes alone showed that humanity

had long left the creature before him.

They continued walking through the wasteland. Marcos

watched McDaniel walk past him, his pace quickened as he looked

around in a searching manner. As if something could be seen on the

bleak horizon around them. The reptilian beast that was Almond did

not notice as McDaniel raised his pistol and took careful, unrushed

aim. McDaniel squeezed the trigger and fired one shot straight

through the center of the beast's back. The reptilian let out a roar of

pain and anger as it fell to its knees. Marshall, roused by the shot, let

out a yelp of fright as he rolled off the shoulder of the reptile and

into the sticky mud. Marcos was frozen with indecision as

everything seemed to slow down around him.

Marshall tried to get up and away from the wounded beast but a large, clawed hand slashed out, striking him full in the face. Droplets of blood fanned out through the air, and Marshall fell backwards, sinking beneath the shallow water. Only his face appeared above the water. Deep, red cuts ran across his face, blood flowing from the wounds. His eyes were closed, giving a deceptively peaceful appearance to his mangled face.

"Marshall!" shouted Marcos as he snapped out of his stunned state. The immense beast that was once Almond turned to face them. The exit wound on its chest from the bullet was a deep, red pool, spilling blood down the bare, scaly chest. Another shot ripped through the air sending the beast staggering as it started to charge at them. It quickly regained its feet and, in two large steps, closed the gap between them.

Marcos raised his hands to shield himself when he heard another shot fired from McDaniel. Warm blood splattered across Marcos's arms along with some chunks of meat and flesh. He lowered his arms and saw that the third shot had hit it right above its right eye and carved out a chunk of its skull. It slowly sank to its knees and toppled over on its side, finally unmoving.

The beastly form of Almond barely sunk below the shallow water, a mountain of scaly muscle and bone rising out of the water. McDaniel gave it one good kick. Satisfied, he grabbed Marcos's arm and started dragging him off in a different direction than they had been traveling. Marcos pulled back and tried to dig in his heels. "Wait! We have to help Marshall," he said as he feebly fought against McDaniel's greater strength.

"We have to move," McDaniel said in a calm steady voice. "They are all linked. They will be coming here soon." He yanked so hard on Marcos's arm that their heads nearly collided as Marcos lost his footing and fell towards him. Marcos saw a desperation in McDaniel's dark eyes, not panic but an awareness of a real danger if they stayed any longer. An anger welled up in Marcos at the callous nature of the man. He started to try and open a rift but could not feel the power that had come so natural on earth. A confusion crossed his face, and he saw a smirk touch the corner of McDaniel's mouth.

"You tried to open a doorway, didn't you? I could see it in your eyes." McDaniel turned away walking at a quick pace, dragging Marcos along. "A doorway can only be opened from the other side and would take tremendous strength to leave open on this side."

"Then what is the rift we walked through to get here?" Marcos asked, "Who holds that open?"

"This place," said McDaniel in a casual tone and showing no signs of becoming winded from the fast pace he was setting, "Is a creation of the First, as you know. A place beyond our world and reality. They have found a way to keep it open through a child. A human one."

Marcos thought he had misheard him. "I thought I heard a child before entering the rift. How is this possible?"

"The first human to come into contact with the First was a child. A young girl, who is currently holding the door, or rift as you may say, between this place and our world. She has held it open for years." McDaniel had sped up to a jog as he kept moving and talking at the same time. He was in peak shape, and with his iron grip on Marcos. He made him keep up. "Years ago, a rescue operation was underway here in the Ozarks for a lost child. They searched for days and finally found some of her belongings at the mouth of a small cave entrance. The team descended and deep within came upon a shimmering, black hole. It was the very doorway that we entered to get here. Those that entered never returned, so the remaining team members returned to the surface and soon the U.S. military built a facility here to study and contain this phenomenon."

McDaniel paused in his story and studied the landscape around them before moving on again. He had let go of Marcos. Marcos thought of fleeing but at this point where would he go? "I was appointed as commander of the base, and it was not long before the scratching began to reach my mind." He abruptly stopped and looked at Marcos with a searching stare. "You know the scratching?"

Marcos only nodded his reply. He knew the scratching that raked at his skull for that long month of working at the base all too well. It had driven him to the edge of madness. As if thinking about it had awoken something, Marcos felt a single spike of pain in his head. It was faint and distant but it was there, as if a probe had been sent out to find him. He saw McDaniel stiffen as the same scratch must have passed through his mind at that moment. The hunt for them had begun.

McDaniel said, "They have called all their most loyal subjects here, along with the most powerful humans they have found, such as yourself. They mean to take over your bodies but need you as willing hosts. They have found that forcing the merging, or ascending as the human followers call it, leads to insanity and unpredictable behavior."

"So they need people like Almond," added Marcos, "How do they plan to make us willing?"

McDaniel made a grimace as he answered, "Any way they can. Offerings of power, threats of pain and torture. Whatever it takes."

Marcos had never felt such hopelessness. "How can we possibly stop this if they have already gathered everyone? What can possibly be done?"

McDaniel leaned in close to Marcos as they continued to slog through the swamp. "They have made many mistakes. Their trust in me is their greatest. With all their most powerful humans and Ascended gathering here, the only way back to the real world is through the doorway the girl keeps open. We get her out and close it, they are trapped, for a while. They will eventually seek out others with power, reaching their minds across the void between their realm and earth. It will be up to us to hunt others with the power and get them on our side, or put an end to them. I also have stopped the Pale One from getting his chosen vessel by stealing you away."

Marcos could see that it was not all as simple as McDaniel was making it out to be. They would have to find this child and then make their way all the way back to the doorway. And, if they managed that, they would have to launch an international hunt for anyone with the power. *How would that even be possible?* He had no idea. McDaniel moved ahead of him, signaling an end to the questions. But Marcos had to ask one more. "Why did you shoot Charles? Why not help us kill Almond back at the doorway?" McDaniel did not turn around and seemed at first that he would not answer. When he spoke, his voice was cold and calculating as his actions had been.

"Your friend had a gun, and I was taking no chances. I also couldn't risk the beast killing me so I had to wait for a better moment to kill it. I will need someone as powerful as you to fight the First. We are in a fight for the survival of our entire species. I will not risk losing this chance to stop them." He pushed on ahead making it clear he was done talking.

Time was meaningless in the First's realm. The pale light that filled the sky neither grew nor wavered. Marcos looked up at the white sky that could have been mistaken for a thick overcast of clouds, but he knew it was not. It was more like being on the inside of an egg; a pure white dome that could have been miles high or only a few hundred feet above him, he could not tell. The sky, like the landscape, was stark and featureless. Yet, as they moved along through the ankle deep waters he saw the first change in geography appear before him. The thin, dead trees that covered the swamp were giving way to large, hollowed out trees that stood upon mounds of grey mud. The mounds were a thousand islands in a murky, warm sea.

"She is here," McDaniel gestured with his pistol towards one of the larger mounds that had a dozen hollow trees dotting it. The mound rose out of the water a few feet but the thick, sticky mud made ascending it a difficult task for Marcos's water-logged sneakers. McDaniel quickly traversed up through the mud, not giving Marcos a single consideration or bit of assistance. Marcos felt a panic building in him as the glue-like mud barely gave way as he used his hands to help pull himself up the small slope. He feared he was trapped here, in a land of mud and pale light. He knew only an hour or so at most had passed since they had entered through the rift, but it felt like days.

McDaniel disappeared behind the trees, and for a moment, Marcos was truly alone. As he stood leaning against one of the hollow trees, looking down at his mud-filled shoes, he heard a child's voice. It had a quaver to it that touched Marcos's heart with its sadness. McDaniel guided her to him, his large hand resting on her thin shoulder. She was thin and frail with matted blonde hair that clung wetly to her face and back. He saw the sadness that filled her voice also touched her large, watery blue eyes.

"Who is he?" she asked McDaniel. Marcos smiled at her to try and lessen her fear, but she continued to look at him uncertainly as her eyes darted around, searching the horizon for danger. "Are we going? They will be here soon."

"How do you know that?" asked Marcos as he nervously stole glances around, expecting to see the First charging at them from the milky mist that was settling over the waters. He saw that McDaniel had a nervous look on his face, the first clear emotion he had seen from him.

The girl responded, "I can always feel him. He lives in my head, making me keep the door open. He keeps me from the others as they will hurt me. They are all mad." She paused and started looking around in a panic." They are here, they are here, they are here," she kept repeating as her hands went to stop an unseeable pain echoing in her mind. A low growl started reverberating in the mist, a rumbling rattling through the air that Marcos could feel in his body. It reminded him of the noise alligators make on nature shows. It was a deep, rhythmic bellow. He looked out into the mist that was moving in and saw the forms of dozens of the First moving towards them. Their throats visibly vibrated as they continued to make the growling in unison. The water rippled and jumped up from the shock of the sound.

Anger filled McDaniel's voice as he cursed, "Dammit, we were too slow." He picked up the girl who quickly buried her face in his chest as she clung to him, her entire body shivering. Marcos figured she was ten or eleven but she was so skinny and frail that

McDaniel seemed to not notice her added weight. McDaniel looked at Marcos and said, "We have to get back. If not, we have to make sure that doorway is closed, at least that will buy more time for anyone resisting back on earth. Do you know what that means?" Marcos was not fully sure he wanted to know but McDaniel continued, "None of us can live. You have to make sure you die and I will take care of us. Now, run!" He quickly pushed Marcos forward toward the direction they had just come.

The sound of the First racing towards them through the shallow water filled him with fear. He could feel his heart beating in his chest as he leapt from the mound to come tumbling down into the waters below. He scrambled to his feet to see several reptilian monsters bounding towards him from his left and right, leaving a small exit between them. He heard McDaniel curse and then the sound of shots rang out from his pistol. Marcos ran with every ounce of strength he had left but could not imagine how he would keep it up for long. A large, greenish, black reptilian was closing in fast on his right. Its outstretched claws reached for him. A guttural hiss escaped its wide split snout as it prepared to latch on to him, and rip and tear at him. He was nearly through the gap when he tripped over a rotten root that sent him sprawling forward just as the monstrous creature lunged for him. The reptile went flailing over him as Marcos fell under the water. The warm water filled his nose and ears, and his hands sank deep into the mud. He thought for a second of letting himself drown, letting all the fear and fatigue drift away in the warm water. The moment passed as a stinging pain reached his mind. He pushed out of the water gasping for air. The scratching in his head had begun again, with long, deep scrapes that dulled his mind. He turned and saw McDaniel was nearly upon him, closely followed by two more of the immense beasts. The water was turning red where two of the reptiles had been shot in the face and lay floating lifeless in it. McDaniel shouted, "Get up! Move! Move! Move!" as he ran past him putting a bullet in the creature that had jumped over Marcos. Marcos got to his feet and started running after them, his legs numb from exertion.

Charles Chenard was bleeding badly. The bullet wound in his right shoulder was radiating fiery pain. He gripped his pistol tightly in his left hand as he fought for every step in the endless swamps, he found himself in. At first, he could see the faint outlines of Marcos, Marshall, and his would-be killers but as he struggled on, they faded from view. Luckily, the waters were so still and the land undisturbed that he was able to continue by following the ripples of the water and the faint tracks in the mud.

He blamed himself. It was a trap and he had known it, yet he had led them into it. They'd left him for dead and that was the only positive he could take from the current situation. He would catch up and kill their attackers. He had been given a second chance and he meant to do something with it. He quickened his pace in the hopes of catching them.

He was sped along even faster after hearing gunshots rip through the stagnant air. He soon found the aftermath of those gunshots as he came upon the reptilian beast that had cut off their exit in the base. He kept his gun trained on its bleeding head as he approached and kicked it. He looked around trying to find a clue as to what had happened. *Who killed you?* He wondered to himself. It had to be the soldier that had shot him but why turn on his own?

An electric current of fear made his muscles seize up, and his breath shortened at the sight of a bloody figure floating face up in the water. He yelled out, "Marshall!" The panic in his own voice scared him. He dropped to his knees and with his left arm pulled Marshall's head out of the water to rest on his thighs. Marshall's left cheek had four long deep cuts slashing across his face from ear to lips. Blood and sticky mud were caked in a long sheet across his cheek. Charles could feel Marshall's shallow breathing against his legs and let out a sigh of relief.

"Marshall, come on, man. Wake up," he said softly as he gently rocked him. Marshall's eyes slowly opened at Charles's words.

"Charles? How are you alive?" Marshall mumbled the words as he struggled to talk from his deep facial wounds. "I saw you die."

Charles let out a soft laugh, "Well, I just thought I saw you dead, so we are even." He helped Marshall to a sitting position. He wanted to give Marshall more time to gather himself but every fiber of his being knew that was a luxury that did not exist. "Where is Marcos? Where did they go?"

Marshall shook his head and gave a fearful glance at the reptilian form of Almond only a few feet away. "I passed out after that freak carried me into this place. Its grip on my throat strangled me. When I awoke, it was to the sound of a gun and then I tumbled off the beast's shoulder. I briefly saw the soldier holding his gun towards the beast with Marcos beside him. Then, this happened." He lightly pointed toward his face. "It backhanded me and that was it."

"Did he say his name or did you over hear it?"

Marshall shook his head gently, "No, I was out then when I awoke, I was already being attacked. Do you think he was rescuing Marcos from them?"

Charles was not so sure. "Why did he shoot me then? Something doesn't add up here. But we can't leave Marcos." Charles stared out across the bleak swampland. "And likely we can't leave without his help. Marshall, we have to follow them. Can you walk?" Marshall pushed himself up, and together they awkwardly made it to their feet. A small, defeated part of Charles wanted to lay down under the warm water and just give up. He was bone-tired, but he started walking off in the direction of the two sets of mud indentations he found going away from their location.

They had only gone a few yards when they heard a gunshot followed by several more. They paused next to a Y-shaped tree that stuck out of the ground about seven feet, wet and decaying. Marshall was holding his head with a pained expression etched into his face. Charles reached out to check on him. Marshall threw up what little was in his stomach and slumped against the tree.

"Marshall," said Charles softly, "You have a bad concussion. I would let you rest here, but I can't trust that I will be able to find you again."

Marshall nodded his head slightly as he wiped his mouth. His voice was raw and scratchy from the retching as he said, "I can keep up. I feel better after that. Just a splitting headache now." He tried for a smile, but Charles could see right through it to the pain behind it. Marshall stopped trying to hide his pain as he asked, "Those gunshots. Do you think Marcos and the soldier were attacked by the beasts?"

"I would imagine..." Charles trailed off as he saw two figures running raggedly towards them. They were human and many monstrous creatures followed in close pursuit. He saw the first figure was the soldier, who was turning and firing into the pursuing tide of monsters. He could make out Marcos trailing slightly behind the soldier. "It's them! and the soldier is carrying a child?" The sentence made little sense to him even as he said it.

"We gotta run, Charles!" Marshall was pulling on his arm back towards the way they had come. "Those monsters are going to run right over us!"

Charles barely registered Marshall's words as he waved his hand to catch Marcos and the soldier's attention. It worked as the two veered directly for them. The child dropped down from her hold on the soldier's neck and yelled out, "Stop here! I can bring it closer! Stop them, McDaniel!" She rushed past Charles and Marshall without barely a recognition of their existence, then closed her eyes and began to strain with outstretched arms so hard a blood vessel stuck out on her forehead from her great effort.

Marcos ran right up to Marshall and Charles and fell at their feet, completely spent. He breathlessly said, "I... I was sure...I was sure you both were dead." He finally managed the words as he gripped his side, his breathing fast and ragged. Charles was completely lost and started to speak but was cut off by Marcos who still holding his side stood back up. "She is the one keeping the rift open that we came through. She is...she's connected to the First. She is somehow bringing the rift closer to us." More shots rang out as McDaniel unloaded his clip and then slammed a new, fully loaded one into his gun. Charles moved up alongside McDaniel and held his gun out towards the couple dozen reptilians standing before them. One lay dead in the water which had given pause to the rest.

McDaniel spoke without looking at Charles, "They are fanning out, trying to encircle us. She had better be quick."

Charles gave him a sideways glance and said, "Bet you're glad your shot didn't kill me. You know if you were on our side you could have helped us from the beginning."

McDaniel shook his head and replied, "I did what I did to secure all of the most important assets of the First. You were an unknown with a gun. I couldn't take the chance." He fired a shot at an approaching reptilian which missed its head by an inch but gave the creature pause. "They will only hold back for a little while. Once more of them have shown up they will rush us."

"Well, hopefully, the girl gets that rift here." Marshall turned around and could see a black sphere hovering over the water, rushing towards them. It felt like a dream, and he had to remind himself this all was actually happening. He looked back towards the growing numbers of the First and saw several humans among them.

"They are the Ascended," said McDaniel, "Likely taken over by the First while they awaited the arrival of Marcos."

"Why do they want Marcos?" asked Charles.

McDaniel answered in a far calmer voice than Charles felt possible considering the situation, "He is the most powerful human they have encountered. I am dwarfed by his power. So, the Pale One has decided he will be his." He stopped abruptly and became rigid. Charles followed his gaze and saw what had given him pause. A bluish, white reptilian was hovering just behind several of the First that stood out before them. Its long, thin arms were outstretched at its sides, and its feet skimmed over the water.

Screams suddenly cut through the air. Charles flinched away from McDaniel as he reached for his head, holding his temples as an agonizing scream escaped from him. Charles looked back and saw Marcos and the girl suffering similar fates. The spherical rift or doorway was only a few yards behind them.

"Marshall, grab the girl, and run for the rift! Go, now!" Charles shouted as loud as he could to be heard over the screams. Charles fired at the Pale One as he walked backwards, but a reptilian in front of it took all the shots and kept standing, held up by those around it. He saw an emotion of terror in the emerald green eyes of the reptilian he had shot and realized it was Alexander. They had used the poor, crazed man as a shield. He had no more time to contemplate the tragedy of Alexander's fate as he was being rushed from his sides by more reptilians. He fired the rest of his ammo widely and started pushing Marcos towards the rift.

Marshall had gotten the girl through the doorway and was running back to get them. McDaniel sped past Charles and Marcos, one hand pressed against his head as he charged forward with great big strides. Charles handed Marcos to Marshall and picked up his own pace to reach McDaniel and get inside the doorway with him. A terrifying thought of McDaniel shooting the girl and sealing them all in this place with the First filled his mind. He tripped at the edge and landed hard on his knees through the doorway. The feeling of solid concrete was a welcome sensation after the endless swamp he had been in. He quickly jumped to his feet and looked for McDaniel. The man had not gone far as he stood checking the girl then looking back into the doorway.

Charles saw Marshall pulling Marcos along, only a few feet from the doorway. Behind them the Pale One and his fellow reptilians were nearly upon them. Charles started to reach through the gateway when he saw McDaniel raise his gun towards Marcos and Marshall. Charles pivoted on his feet and launched himself at McDaniel knocking him down and falling alongside him. Charles landed on his bad right arm and nearly blacked out from the pain. McDaniel was yelling, "No! They can't get him. They can't have him." He fired a shot into the doorway. Charles wanted to yell a warning but it was all happening so fast. He saw Marcos trip and pull Marshall back and in front of him. The bullet hit Marshall in the stomach sending him crashing backwards the rest of the way.

The girl yelled out, "I can't hold it any longer! He's too close!"

One instant Charles was watching his two friends becoming enveloped in a tide of scaly flesh and claws and then the next there was nothing. A bare stone wall stood behind a steel door frame; whose solid steel door stood wide open. The hallway was lit by pale fluorescent lightbulbs and only the sounds of the girl's sobs filled the room. This was broken by the shouts of McDaniel at her. "Damn you! Damn you, both! Now, they have him! The Pale One will take over his body in time and then find another way into our world!"

The girl was sobbing on the floor, her clothes sopping wet and hair still matted. "I tried! He was hurting my head so bad; I just couldn't keep it open. He was there helping me keep it open one moment then gone the next. He wanted it closed." She spoke pleadingly to them. Charles managed to get to his knees and scoot over to her.

"It's okay, now," he managed to say. "You are safe now." He couldn't believe he found the words or even was able to say them with genuine feeling. McDaniel let out a loud scoff at the words and turned towards them. His pistol was pointed at the ground, but Charles could see he longed to raise it and shoot them.

"No one is safe," McDaniel said through gritted teeth. "We have a war going on here. I have men fighting all over this continent to find anyone with the power to open more doorways and the cult followers of the First. For all they need is to find one more like Marcos or me. Once they find that person all they need is for Marcos to become Ascended."

"He'll fight it," said Charles defiantly.

McDaniel stared at him for a moment before saying, "I hope that is true. For he must be a willing host for it to be a successful ascending. We will know. In time, we will know. Now, we must stop everything I helped start." He walked past them and down the hallway.

"What's your name?" Charles asked as he helped her up as best, he could with one arm.

"Sarah...Sarah Caldern." She paused in thought for a moment then said, "Why didn't you shoot him?" She lightly touched the pistol still in his hand.

He placed it back in its holster. "Out of ammo." He considered the look on her face and decided it was from disappointment. "He will get his. But, for now, we have to stay alive to make that happen. And then find a way to rescue my friends."

"Yes," she said in a tired voice. Her eyes were swollen from crying. "I really didn't mean to leave your friends there. I... I wouldn't wish that place on anybody." He rubbed her back gently and started walking. He had to get them back but how? He looked at the girl and knew she was the key to it. He would get them back and finish that Pale One and McDaniel as violently as he could.

Project Ostium X: Despair and Hope

News of the Nation anchor David Huan's voice filled the dark hotel room. His normally calming cadence was missing from days of reporting on the chaos gripping the United States. *"Our News of the Nation chopper is on the scene now as combat continues around Chicago and the surrounding area. For the safety of the crew they are staying far back from the frontline, but as we have seen over the past several weeks, no one can be sure where the frontline is at any given time. Let's go now to Sandra Valdez, Sandra?"*

Blackness descended across the sparsely furnished room as the television went dark during the cutaway. White light danced back along the wall and the queen-sized bed as Sandra Valdez's face filled the screen. Fear filled her eyes as she struggled to gather herself and be heard over the whirling blades of the chopper. *"David, we are seeing a sprawling front of tanks and men battling to reach the south side of the city. Our loyalist forces have been hammering the rebel positions for hours with artillery pieces into the neighborhoods on the northside of Interstates 94 and 294. We are just over Brownell Woods and can see all of the residential areas north of it are simply leveled from the bombardment. This kind of attack is occurring all around us. It's a terrifying sight Nathan. Just terrifying."*

The din of noise abated as the news channel quickly cut back to David. *"Stay safe Sandra, and same to our brave troops fighting the rebel forces that have sprung up all over our country from within our own military. Now, let's go to Burt Bulford in our New of the Nation Crisis Center who can give us more insight into the five nuclear detonations that have occurred in four different cities. Burt?"*

"David, we have finally had confirmation from a nuclear facility outside of San Diego that confirms a dozen nuclear missiles were taken before the base could be secured by loyalist forces. So far, Los Angeles, Kansas City, New York City, and Atlanta have been victims of these monstrous bombs. New York received the worst of it with two separate explosions just days apart. No connection has been made as to why these cities in particular were chosen other than they are representative of different regions across the U.S. Perhaps an insidious message that no one is safe. And, until the other seven bombs can be found, that will be a very true statement."

Huan filled the television screen again. *"Thanks, Burt. I just received word that we have breaking news images of the cities that have been devastated by the nuclear attacks. We warn our viewers the following images of the nuclear attacks are disturbing."* The pale, gaunt hand of Charles Chenard pressed the off button on the side of the television. The room became pitch dark but was soon broken up by the pale orange and yellow lights that filtered in through the drawn curtains. Charles went to the window and pushed open the curtains to look out on a nearly empty Memphis, Tennessee. The fear of another nuclear attack had driven most people from the cities, or as in the case of Chicago, the very real threat of the warring armies that swept across the continent.

It had been a month since he had escaped the military compound in the Ozarks. He had gone in with Marshall and Marcos, and come out with a young girl named Sarah Caldern and the man responsible for all that has occurred, Colonel Nathan McDaniel. The bastard had Sarah taken away to some hidden facility and made it clear that her wellbeing rested on Charles's silence and cooperation. The weeks had gone by and Charles had to stand by and watch the world he knew fall apart. A civil war between the military had broken out all over the country as the First's supporters corrupted and manipulated entire divisions of the U.S. Army to make them turn. The infiltration by the First into all levels of government and military was staggering. Charles had seen enough atrocities over the past weeks to last him a lifetime. And he knew it was all thanks to Colonel McDaniel and his playing of both sides against each other. The man had staged the U.S. military into a civil war at the behest of the First, and now an entire continent was reaping the fruits of that evil.

Charles knew he had grown paranoid of late. Three times he had Ascended, humans that have had the First transferred into them through unknown means, come to kill him. The result of this Ascending is always the same, a slow takeover of the mental and physical form of the human until they are transformed into a sentient, reptilian horror. Often these are people of power and standing that can go anywhere they need to before the transformation becomes obvious. Charles, with the help of Colonel McDaniel's ever-present special forces that watch and guard him, took down all three assassins. He trusted no one now.

Yet, here he was waiting in a hotel room all because he had received an anonymous text stating, "Marcos is alive. We have to meet." What a clumsy trap. Charles was almost impressed with the unsubtle boldness of this latest assassination attempt on his life. The other times he had been tricked and thrown off by calls or messages from CIA operatives and family members. Those attacks had been unexpected, but he had learned his lesson. Trust no one. Now they were baiting him with his dead former partner. *Was he dead? Can I be so sure?* The thoughts and doubt would not leave his mind no matter how he tried to shake it. It didn't matter whether he did or not. McDaniel, always ready to kill Ascended, was going to make him go into the trap no matter what.

Charles stood in the dark hotel room waiting nervously, knowing that a dozen special forces waited in adjoining rooms to rush in and take out whoever showed up was little comfort as he had nearly died from the previous assassinations on him. McDaniel always leaked his location to the enemy, making any chance of escape from death for Charles a near impossibility. But he had beat the odds and intended to keep beating them.

Charles heard a soft knock at the door and readied himself. He had his gun in his right hand, the arm nearly fully healed from the bullet wound it had sustained. He peered through the peephole and felt his heart sink. The First had finally done it, they found a new way to hurt him. He opened the door slightly and said, "Don't enter until I say." His voice was scratchy as he hadn't spoken out loud in a day. He hardly spoken to anyone anymore. Everyone was suspect; that is the thinking that had kept him alive since the base.

Charles backed up, keeping his gun leveled at the door. The bathroom was on his right and then a thin wall followed by the bed. He found a chair and placed it in the narrow space between the bed and the bathroom wall. He then moved to the far corner of the room where he could keep his pistol trained on the door and the chair, but also stay out of direct view of the window that looked out over the parking lot. He leaned against the wall in the shadows of the room where the street lights did not reach.

"Enter," he commanded. The door slowly creaked open and the pale light of the hallway outlined the figure of Marshall Dunnett, the friend he had left behind. Charles's insides twisted with panic at the sight.

"Walk forward slowly and sit in the chair. Very slowly." His words were filled with the tension he felt inside. His friend silently walked forward, the hotel room door pulling shut behind him, and sat in the chair, a hesitation in his steps as he moved. He could see a visible shake in his legs as he walked. Marshall was terrified. "What is this?" Charles asked, a menace to his voice to hide his own fear at what he was seeing.

Marshall was partially illuminated by the orange and yellow street lights as he sat with his hands gripping his knees, his back straight against the seat. Charles could see his eyes sparkling in the light. They were normal human eyes. "I have been looking for you for days. They let me go, so I knew I had to find you as soon as I could." Marshall's words were fast and clipped. He shifted restlessly in his seat as he spoke.

"They just let you go? Why?" Charles spoke slowly, hoping to calm Marshall if not himself.

"I... I was no use to them. They told me over and over again. After I was shot by McDaniel and the rift closed, they carried us off. That pale reptile removed the bullet and healed me. There were dozens of those reptilian beasts and people there, too. The people were questioning me. They hurt me." His words faltered and he started taking great gasps of air. Charles saw it was a panic attack. He wanted to rush over and comfort his friend, but he knew better. If he learned anything over these past weeks it was not to give in, not to let your guard down.

"Marshall, I need you to take off your shirt." Charles's words were ice. He made himself as removed from them as he could.

As Marshall struggled to get his breathing under control his face flushed, losing all color to it. "No, Charles, listen to me. They did terrible things. I couldn't help it. They can break you, anyone." His words trailed off as he started fidgeting even more, stealing glances out the window through the parted curtains.

Charles did what he never dreamed of doing. He raised his gun and leveled it directly at Marshall's head. He said, "Take off the shirt. Now." He cocked the hammer back and was surprised by how his hand was not shaking. He flicked his eyes towards the window then back at Marshall. "Are you expecting someone else?"

Marshall did not answer but unbuttoned and removed the flannel shirt he was wearing. Underneath the flannel he had a white t-shirt that he pulled over his head slowly, as if it hurt to move in such a way. Charles's darkest suspicions were realized. Along the sides and stomach of Marshall's body his skin had patches of raw, red flesh outlining tiny, leathery scales. The scaly skin was dark green but glistened in the light, wet and new. Marshall moved his hands instinctively to cover his deformed flesh, but it was too large of an area to cover, and the damage had been done.

"Marshall." It was all Charles could manage. He said his friend's name in sadness and disappointment. McDaniel had told him that the First had learned that forcing the Ascending transformation led to madness for the host. They had been strictly practicing willing conversions ever since. Charles stared at his friend down the barrel of a gun knowing that he had willingly given himself over to the First.

Marshall leaned forward in his chair; arms outstretched towards Charles as he pleaded with him. "They said if I allowed the Ascending, they would stop hurting me and Marcos. They said they can reverse it. As long as I helped them. I lasted as long as I could but…" His words trailed off, his lips quivering as they tried to form more words but none came.

"Marshall, I am so sorry. I won't go to them. They have lied to you to get to me. You fucked up bad, Marshall. I can't help you." Charles wanted to tell his friend to run, to get out before all hell came crashing down on them. But he knew there was nowhere for Marshall to go now.

Marshall fell to his knees, his hands still outstretched to Charles as he leaned against the bed. He winced in pain as the raw skin of his stomach touched the abrasive comforter on the bed. "Don't give up on Marcos. He still holds out. They can't hurt him like they did me. They need him intact." Shadows moved across the room as several figures passed in front of the window. A crash rang out and the hotel's fire exit door alarm started blaring. Marshall's words spilled out of him as he spoke quickly, "Charles, they mean to find Marcos's parents. They want to capture them and use them to make Marcos give in. You have to get to them before they do. They are somewhere in Indiana but that's all I know."

Charles moved out from his corner to move closer to Marshall. He kept the gun trained on Marshall's head as he moved next to Marshall, keen to keep his body against the bathroom wall to expose as little of himself as possible to the door and anyone coming through it. Marshall lightly placed his hands-on Charles's leg and said, "Please, Charles. Don't let me become like Alexander. It is too painful. Make it stop." Marshall closed his eyes and eased his forehead up to the gun. Charles was more horrified that he was not more resistant to Marshall's request. Marshall had not been an easy companion, but he was his closest friend. Charles heard voices at the closed door and the unmistakable sound of metal sliding against leather as guns were drawn from holsters. He looked down at Marshall and said, "I'm sorry I ever got you involved in this." His finger gave a slight twitch, and the gun recoiled sharply. Marshall rocked back against the arm of the chair, blood and skull splattering the floor and wall behind him. He slumped over with eyes closed and mouth open.

Charles looked away from what he had done, repeating to himself that he did not have time to think about it, and crouched down against the wall as he heard the beep of a keycard unlocking the door and then it flew open. First, he saw the barrel of a handgun appear then the man holding it cleared the wall and was standing directly in front of him. From Charles's crouched perspective he was just a formless shape by the side of the bed in the black room as the man scanned the far wall. Charles pointed his gun and fired at the man's head. The man went reeling sideways into the television stand and wall, falling limply to the ground. Then, all hell broke loose. The window shattered inwards as a smoke grenade flew through it, slamming into the second person to enter as they stumbled over the fallen body of the first one. Charles fired another shot into the midriff of that man. A spray of bullets from the street filled the room, and the door to the adjoining hotel room came swinging open and two-gun barrels poked through, unloading more gunfire into the confusion. Charles was choking on smoke and found his eyes and ears overwhelmed from the gunshots and muzzle flashes. He could tell that several of the attackers had jumped into the bathroom just past the front door as his own "team members" fired from the adjoining door and the street. More gunshots echoed from the parking lot as a gun battle erupted between both sides' arriving reinforcements.

Charles turned on his heels in his crouched position and realized he was boxed in by the chair with Marshall's dead body and the bed. He started crawling over the bed as fast as he could to get back towards the relative safety of the far corner of the room. The special forces in the adjoining doorway called a command to the soldiers right outside the window to cease fire. Then, in perfect unity, they entered the room and charged the bathroom. The first soldier went down under a flurry of gunfire. The second soldier had a grenade already primed and tossed it into the bathroom as he retreated back. The explosion went off with a deafening bang. The soldier, that threw the grenade, rushed into the bathroom firing a spray of bullets with his machine gun. He called the all clear and a stark silence fell in the room broken only by the sound of gunfire from the parking lot. Charles had just reached the far end of the room next to the window when Colonel McDaniel entered from the adjoining room. The smoke grenade's choking cloud had mostly dissipated, settling in a fine haze just above the ground.

McDaniel gave a curious glance to Marshall's crumpled form in the chair and then gave a twisted smile to Charles as he said, "What have we done to you?" His laugh was sickening to hear, yet despite the ringing in his ears, Charles heard it. It was a mirthless bark more than laughter and died out as quickly as it had started.

Charles ripped off the small microphone he had taped to his chest under his shirt and tossed it at McDaniel's feet. "Did you hear what he said? Marcos is still there, resisting. And they mean to go after his parents."

McDaniel removed his earpiece that was connected to Charles's microphone. He had a look of annoyance on his face at the microphone being thrown to the ground causing the sound to reverberate in his ear. He replied, "Of course he is still fighting them. They would be storming across the country, swallowing all before them with their power if he had Ascended and returned. His parents though, that is a complication. Not sure I can trust anyone to get them without us there." A grenade blast rang out from the parking lot. The raging battle was drawing closer. McDaniel motioned for Charles to follow him. "Time to go. Sounds like they are throwing more than just these few guys at us to get to you." Charles felt a small sense of satisfaction at the concerned look that crossed McDaniel's face as he looked through the blown-out window. The Pale One had cut the link to McDaniel and Sarah which had left them both unable to use their powers.

Charles stared down McDaniel as they moved into the hall. McDaniel said, "What are you looking at?"

"A turtle without his shell. You aren't very useful without your powers, are you?"

McDaniel answered in a cold, calm voice, "My powers will return. I can feel them; I just can't reach them because of the Pale One." He paused as they reached the exit door at the end of the hallway. The special forces soldiers moved ahead of them to check outside. "How about your friend back there? You did what I would've done. He was only good for getting in the way."

Charles knew better than to rise to the bait. Still, he felt loathed to imagine his actions could ever be compared to McDaniel's. He held his tongue as he had learned quickly that McDaniel fed on verbal conflict and seeing others become upset. He would always bring up failures or insults to get a reaction out of others to then just tear them down further. Arguing was a waste of breath and Charles had gotten the dig in that he had wanted. The sound of gunshots ripping through the hotel at the other end of the hallway drew his attention back to the real danger they were still in. He was glad that the hotel was mostly empty. He had seen enough collateral damage these past weeks to last a lifetime.

"Go, go, go!" shouted one of the soldiers at the door and they raced into an armored black Humvee and sped off. The sounds of gunfire died away as they made it to the highway and out of the city. Charles closed his eyes and tried to rest despite McDaniel barking orders over the phone. He quickly had to open his eyes again as an image of Marshall's dead body filled his mind. He knew that sleep was going to be hard to come by for a long time.

It took days to reach Indiana. Roads of rubble and cities of ruin were all that greeted the lone Humvee as it made its way north. Charles told himself he would be numb to the horrors they would see. But, his heart was filled with sadness at the sight of battlefields of burning tanks and mutilated bodies, and fires raging in the distance as entire forests burned from indiscriminate bombings. The entire military was in a massive civil war that raged without clear boundaries or safe havens. McDaniel had infiltrated the military with his cult of the First and twisted thousands of minds through his lies and promises. The irony was that he had switched sides near the end of all of his well laid plans, and needed to use forces loyal to him and have them fight back against all those that held allegiance purely to the ideals of the First he had planted in them. It was a nightmare that Charles, and the country, could not wake from. How could so many be deceived to the point that they would kill their own fellow soldiers and Americans? Charles knew it spoke to a fickleness that lay in most, a cowardice to follow orders and go with the majority around them even if it meant committing atrocities. But the fact that a civil war was occurring proved that many others could not be swayed so easily.

To add to the confusion that gripped the nation was the sight of reptilian beasts leading soldiers, showing them the power and strength that they could achieve. The power was blocked from these beasts as it was for McDaniel and Sarah, likely due to whatever method the Pale One was using to subdue it, but all had seen what they were capable of as entire tanks were swallowed up through rifts, or jets flying into a rift formed in the sky. Both would enter the realm of the First disoriented and quickly become stuck or crash outright into that boggy swampland, only to be picked apart by the prepared monsters waiting.

"We are close," McDaniel said loudly over the constant radio chatter. "A trusted informant has found them just outside Fort Wayne, Indiana. They apparently fled to a family member's house to escape their home city of Buffalo, New York; which is nothing more than a ruin now. But Fort Wayne has escaped most of the conflict. Should be as easy as going up to their front door and knocking."

Charles felt rage build up inside him at the dismissive tone of McDaniel describing what they had seen over the past days as a 'conflict'. *What a simple clean word,* thought Charles. He felt holocaust and apocalypse were more accurate words. Indianapolis was a bombed-out ruin that they had to skirt around to avoid swarms of desperate refugees who clogged the roads, unsure where they could go as the war raged around them.

The house Marcos Romano's parents had fled to was a simple, one-story brick home in a suburb on the outskirts of Fort Wayne. They pulled over and stopped three houses away, and everyone started to check their weapons and gear before leaving the Humvee. Charles had traveled with McDaniel and four special forces operatives. These men were not about to get caught off guard by the peaceful neighborhood. In fact, it seemed to Charles that this just made everyone more tense, himself included. They quickly moved to the house, everyone scanning for the attack that was sure to come.

"This has to be a trap somehow," he said softly and saw agreement on everyone's faces.

"Likely," answered McDaniel as if it had been a question. "But we don't have any choice. We can't run the risk of them falling into the hands of the enemy, and if they have, it is best we know." McDaniel motioned for two of the special forces soldiers to go around behind the houses and work their way to the back yard. Everyone else started a slow, cautious walk to the front of the house.

Charles hung back on the sidewalk, looking back and forth across the street for any signs of a trap. McDaniel and two soldiers reached the front door and prepared to bust it down. Charles looked back over his shoulder. The hair on his neck standing straight up as he sensed eyes staring at him. He saw movement behind a large oak tree in the yard across the street. It had been only a brief moment, but he knew he had seen shimmering scales as the noon sun peered through the bare branches of the tree. He raised his gun towards the tree when he heard McDaniel and the soldiers break down the door. A pair of screams from inside the house revealed that Marcos's parents were still in there. He wanted to shout out, but they would never hear him. He heard the attack before he saw it. Heavy clawed feet clicking on the concrete sidewalk from either side of him. He turned to his right and saw a massive green reptilian charging at him. He aimed and fired, taking it in its right hip. The reptilian's wide mouth was open in a scream of rage as it stumbled in its rush to him. He tried to spin but the one from the other direction was on him. An equally large, brown reptilian slammed into his side with immense force sending them both tumbling to the lawn five feet from where he had been standing. His pistol was knocked from his hand and went spinning through the air.

The reptilian and Charles landed on the brown lawn in a heap, both desperately grappling with each other. The beast's warm breath turned his stomach as it opened its wide mouth to bite at his neck. A mouth with rows of razor-sharp teeth snapped at him as he struggled to push it off of him. It was too powerful and had him pinned. He heard the sound of gunshots ringing out in the house and the sound of boots and clawed feet running across the street towards them.

He used his left hand to hold the neck of the beast as his right hand reached into his coat for the small snub-nosed 38 revolver he had put in there previously. He pulled it out just as the clawed hands

pushed his left arm down, and he placed the revolver to the slitted,

green eye of the reptile. He pulled the trigger and felt hot blood

splatter on his face. It dripped into his eyes, momentarily blinding

him.

He struggled to find the strength to push the heavy corpse off

of him but did at last. He rolled over and wiped the blood from his

eyes. He saw his Walther pistol had fallen only a foot from him. As

he picked it up he saw the first reptilian he had wounded was

crawling toward him. He raised the Walther. The green reptilian

hissed at him and it spoke in a rhythmic chant as it crawled. "Hear

the terror of the past. It is a rumble in the chests of those that believe.

A tremor to ripple around the world. Commit now to the way it was,

so it shall be again." Its' words were guttural behind the razor-sharp

teeth and thick reptile tongue but he understood them. They gave

him pause as he listened.

A half dozen shots slammed into the crawling beast, filling

the reptile with smoking holes. The dying beast sank heavily upon

the road, its last wheezing gasps filling its mouth with blood. Charles

turned and saw McDaniel walking towards him holding an H&K

MP5 machine gun, a short stocky gun, with his right hand that he kept trained on the dying creature. McDaniel was covered in blood and breathing heavily. One other special forces soldier was behind him, bleeding profusely from a limp arm that he cradled against his stomach.

"They took them. Must have just happened." McDaniel's words were said haltingly as he tried to control his breathing.

Charles stood up on shaking legs and asked, "What do you mean? I heard them in there."

McDaniel gave an angry stare back at the house, "I don't know who those people were, but they are not them. They must have been younger than me. Neighbors likely captured and tied up to give us pause when we stormed in." He wiped blood from his cheeks; it was starting to congeal in his whiskers. He froze up like a statue and stood staring blankly in the distance. "I feel it, the power."

Charles absentmindedly reloaded his pistol as he said, "They opened a portal, didn't they? They took his parents to their realm."

"We have to move quickly." McDaniel turned to the last soldier, the other three dead or dying inside the house, and said, "Stay here, a relief squad is in-bound by chopper." Before the injured man could reply McDaniel opened a portal to the First's realm. He said without looking at Charles, "We have to go now."

Charles hesitated as he looked at the swirling void. A pale light filled it. One that had haunted his dreams every night since returning, and he knew it would continue to do so. McDaniel walked through without glancing back. Charles just wanted it all to end. Every ounce of his body was tired and aching. He thought of what had happened to Marshall and promised himself that he would put a bullet in his own head before being captured. With a sheer force of will he entered the rift and came crashing down into the warm waters of the dying swamplands. He looked around and saw nothing but the empty waste he remembered, then the empty calm was cut by the piercing screams of people being tortured. He struggled to his feet in the slippery mud as he rushed after McDaniel towards the screams.

Project Ostium XI: Ascension

If Marcos Romano could have figured out how to swallow his tongue and choke to death, he would have done it. Everything had gone wrong, everything had failed, and he knew it was all his fault.

Or was that just more tricks and lies from the First? He couldn't tell the difference anymore. After Marshall had been tortured and given in to Ascension, he saw firsthand how they can break someone, and knew it was only a matter of time before they broke him too. He wondered if Marshall was out amongst the swamp, transforming, or if he was sent back to the real world. Either way it was a cruel fate for Marshall.

The island of slimy mud and rotting trees he found himself upon was not that different from the one that McDaniel and himself had found the girl. "At least she got away," he said out loud to himself. Of course, she was left with Colonel McDaniel, a cold-hearted killer that was just as likely to torture and kill her as the First would.

He longed to feel the power but felt only emptiness. In the realm of the First, the Pale One decided who could wield the power. It would take a person in the real world to reach him but the Pale One had somehow cut everyone off from the power.

He heard the sound of boots moving towards him in the sucking mud and saw his torturer returning. A short man with thin hair and broken glasses appeared before Marcos with a sharp knife in his left hand. Marcos had his back propped up against a tree with his head lolled to one side as he gave the little man a half-interested stare. A laugh escaped Marcos that surprised him as he did not know what was left to laugh about.

"You going to kill me?" said Marcos as another, softer laugh left him unbidden, "That would be okay with me."

The man knelt down at his feet and placed the tip of the knife on his shoe, twirling it slowly, carving out a small whole in the rubber end of the shoe. "I am done with your attitude. You have resisted, and for what? To be driven to the point of suicide? Asking me to kill you so casually?" The man stopped the twirling of the knife and continued, "You are being offered a gift the rest of us would kill our own families for. The Pale One wants you to be his vessel of Ascension and you lay here in despair when you should be on your feet rejoicing!" He plunged the knife between Marcos's knees. Marcos's legs both twitched instinctively away from the blade. The man sneered at him. "Maybe you do still have some will to live after all."

Marcos pulled his legs in up to his body and replied, "Why don't you go kill your family then and leave me alone. I'm never letting him in."

A smile split the small egg-shaped head of the man as he said, "No, I have settled for your family." He stood up and pointed to a commotion in the distance. Marcos slowly turned his head in the direction and saw a group of the First and their human acolytes moving towards them, surrounding something that they were pushing and dragging along. He heard a woman scream and the sound cut through him.

"Mother!" He shouted, then turned back to the man and yelled, "How!? Why!?"

The balding man wiped the knife off on the pale, green trousers he was wearing and licked his lips absentmindedly. "You will Ascend. One way or another...you will Ascend."

The crowd parted as Marcos's parents were pushed to the front and up the steep slope of the island. Everyone had to climb up on their hands and knees to get up the nine-foot incline out of the island. Reptilian horrors lifted and shoved his parents up onto the top of the island. Marcos had gotten to his feet and was about to rush towards them when he was given pause by a figure floating through the air over the crowd, the Pale One.

"Marcos? Marcos what is going on?" pleaded his father, Sal Romano. His father was a thin delicate man of ill health and Marcos could already see the stress affecting his body. His mother, Eliza, clung tightly to her husband's hand, her hair slick with mud, and it stuck to her face in thick clumps. She shivered violently as the Pale One floated past her; one clawed hand outstretched towards her face causing her to recoil in horror.

"Leave them alone!" Marcos shouted at it, but the words came out hollow and feeble. The bald man grabbed his father and yanked him forward while sticking out one short leg and booting his mother to the ground. Sal Romano swung a weak but well aimed punch at the man's ear, rocking the bald man's head. The bald man turned on him as quick as a snake, grabbed his throat with an iron grip, and put the point of the knife to just under Sal's left eye. Eliza cried out as she struggled to her feet but a blueish green Reptilian was upon her and picked her flailing body up into a tight hug.

The bald man spoke through clenched teeth, spit flying from his mouth on to Sal's face. "You strike me again, you old shit, and I will slash open both of your eyes as your family watches, then I'll do their eyes. Got it!" He slid the knife swiftly down Sal's face opening up a shallow cut down his cheek. Sal let out a gasp of shock and pain as blood poured down his face.

Sal spoke in a trembling but defiant voice, "Just kill us and be done with it."

The bald man moved Sal closer to where Marcos stood with his legs shaking from adrenaline and fatigue, his whole body threatening to collapse and sink into the warm mud forever. Marcos was soon close enough to reach out and hold his father's arm which despite the hopeless situation, still provided him some comfort and assurance in its strength. He couldn't understand how a frail old man was able to stand tall despite all that was occurring, and it made him feel shame at his thoughts of death and giving up. *How weak I am*, he thought bitterly to himself.

The Pale One had been floating off to the side, observing the interactions of the humans with cold emotionless lizard eyes. He landed softly on the mud and in a few long strides was standing before Marcos and his father. Its long slender arms hung loosely at its side, showing no fear of the two humans.

Marcos was transfixed by the Pale One. Its dark green, slit pupils stared at him with calculating intelligence behind them. Its muzzle was not as pronounced as the other reptilians and its mouth was a broad row of razor-sharp teeth, slightly open as a pale, grey tongue flicked out towards him. It was a foot taller than him if it had stood upright, but it was hunched over, its eyes level with his.

Marcos saw the images race across his mind. The Pale One communicated only through images; it had used them often when trying to break him. The images were of his parents suffering, he wanted to look away but it did not matter, they were inside his head and there was no way to shake them. He saw his parents flayed alive, and it was himself who held the knife as it sliced through them. The image was clear, any harm that came to them was on him, his stubbornness, his fear.

Sal gripped his hand tightly and Marcos looked into his eyes. Sal said, "I don't know what is going on son, but you can't help us. Find a way to save yourself."

Marcos knew what he had to do. He turned to the bald man and the reptilian holding his mother and said, "You win. Let her go and I will Ascend willingly." The bald man had a look of disappointment on his face but helped ease his mother down from the monstrous arms of the reptilian and then tossed her casually towards Sal. She kept her footing and staggered to the arms of her husband.

Marcos looked at his bewildered parents and said, "I have been running from these monsters for a long time. They want me, need me, for this ancient one to take my body." His parents both started shouting protests but he stopped them by placing his hands on their shoulders and saying softly to them, "I know what I am doing, but when it starts you need to run. I don't know how or where but you need to run and find a way out." He turned from them before he could lose his courage. The fear in his parents' eyes was more than he could stand.

He turned and was face to face with the Pale One. It had stalked closer while he talked with his parents and he felt its long, boney claws close around his arms. He focused his mind and tried to develop images of himself merging with the Pale One. He felt it pulling at the images and he could have sworn he saw the first emotion yet in its eyes, satisfaction.

Charles and McDaniel raced through the swamp at a pace that Charles knew he could not keep up for long. He was about to demand, maybe even beg for a slower pace when McDaniel suddenly stopped dead in his tracks, so fast Charles collided into his back.

"What is it?" Charles asked. He moved around McDaniel and saw his face was frozen as if he were listening to a faint sound in the distance.

"She just spoke to me. Faint but it was her."
Charles cautiously asked, "Sarah? Sarah just contacted you from Earth?" McDaniel nodded his head. He froze up again then a rift opened a few feet away from them and Charles found himself staring into what appeared to be a cafeteria, cold, concrete cafeteria much like one would expect to see in a prison. The young girl, Sarah, that they had rescued from the First's realm, was standing at the front of several dozen people. All of them were dressed in bright orange prison jumpsuits. Several held guns and batons and he noticed several unmoving bodies on the ground and many more subdued men and women sitting beside the large group of people.

Sarah waved to them. She looked different to Charles as she was clean and her blonde hair was tightly braided over one shoulder. Her large eyes had a shocked quality to them that spoke of the horrible things she had witnessed.

McDaniel had a faint smile appear on his face. Only noticeable by his right cheek pulling back to put his mouth in its unnatural pose. "She escaped with the others that have the power. I think I'm finally impressed by her." Charles wanted to knock McDaniel down and smash in his half smile with a muddy boot. The man finally found something that gave him joy and it was a young girl being forced to commit violence. McDaniel continued, "I will tell her to release the guards and send them through with weapons. They may be just what we need to reach Marcos."

"Cannon fodder," said Charles contemptuously.

McDaniel focused on him for a moment, letting his connection with Sarah slip as he replied, "Exactly. And when you come up with a better solution you let me know." His face went blank again as he reached out to Sarah. Soon, Charles was helping guards in military fatigues, armed with an assortment of guns and striking weapons out of the watery mud as they passed through the rift. McDaniel immediately started ordering them to form up and march out before questions could be raised or any kind of organization among them could form. Charles could not think of a better distraction than about twenty armed guards. He soon realized he was wrong on that account.

Colonel McDaniel was fiercely pushing everyone forward with threat and duty. The degree to which McDaniel had these people brainwashed into buying his superiority and authority was amazing to Charles. McDaniel had cultivated a powerful cult of personality in his military personnel and it was clear to Charles how he had started a civil war that raged in the real world. The reality of that ongoing war became very apparent to Charles as he realized the power had been returned to all those on Earth with it. Rifts were opening in the far distance and people and machines were falling through into the First's realm. He could see the smoke rising from tanks and vehicles, the sound of screams and yelling filled the air then were quickly cut off as those people were ambushed and cut down by the First.

"How have they not found us yet?" Charles asked McDaniel as they marched along behind a loose line formed by the prison guards.

"They are distracted by the other arrivals to this realm. They are connected to those First on Earth that are Ascended. Sarah and I are outside that influence for the most part. I am sure that their leader is aware of us but he must be distracted with Marcos. All his will is likely bent towards getting him to Ascend."

"Is that why everyone's powers came back? Because he is distracted?"

McDaniel nodded and answered, "Exactly. And on top of that his forces here are scattered dealing with killing all that enter." He paused in speaking and his face focused again as if on a distant voice. "I can sense him. He feels different, as if his guard is down. He and Marcos must not be far. I feel they are just a little farther ahead amongst those islands that are appearing on the horizon."

Charles saw the approaching clumps of islands and dead trees. He also saw movement on them. He checked his gun to make sure he had a round in the chamber and a full clip. He did not have much ammo and would have to make it count. "Is Marcos giving in? Damn we are so close."

McDaniel yelled at everyone to double time. He said to Charles, "Yes, I think he is Ascending. We can't let it complete or this is all over and we are going to die or be trapped here for all time." Charles was winded but managed to pick up his pace to keep up with the advancing guards. He saw what must have been a hundred reptilians appearing on the edge of the islands with a few human figures dotted amongst them. Any hope in their plan fully faded from his mind as he heard the deep guttural growl that started to resonate from the First. The sound was reverberating everywhere and made his eardrums ring and the water all around them ripple with its effect. McDaniel yelled out, "Fire! Fire, and advance!"

The guards with rifles and pistols opened up on the wall of beasts before them. The guttering stopped as several dropped and the living wall started advancing at them in a dead sprint. The guards in front of Charles parted slightly and he raised his pistol to fire on the reddish monstrosity directly in front of him. He guessed it was now only fifty yards away and closing the distance at an incredible rate. As he pulled his trigger a large, black void appeared above the reptilian's head and a Abrams tank came crashing through, landing atop the reptile, crushing it down into the mud with comical swiftness. Charles back pedaled at the sight, slipped, and went into a slide that sent him down on his butt into the water. He heard McDaniel let out a hysterical laugh at the carnage.

McDaniel yelled out to the fallen Charles, "Sarah is a madwoman! She is dropping everything in from the military prison I put her in!

Get up Charles and stay on my six!" McDaniel ejected his spent clip and slammed home a new one into his pistol as he took off running. The Abrams tank rotated its turret and fired point blank into the mass of reptilians that it had landed amongst sending body parts and mud flying through the air. The wall of beasts was in shambles as more vehicles and soldiers started falling in amongst them. Charles could hardly process the carnage before him as bewildered soldiers fell from the skies amongst equally confused and disoriented reptilians. It was chaos on a level he could not process. The prison guards were scattered, everyone fighting their own personal battle for survival.

Charles followed after McDaniel as he dashed through a gap in the fighting that had just been carved out by the Abrams machine guns. Charles ran hunched down as bullets whizzed through the air; he was focused on his feet and not tripping over the bodies strewn about the shallow waters. They raced on into the islands, McDaniel drawn towards the Pale One and Marcos as if they were a blazing lighthouse amongst a raging, night sea.

The sound of the butchery behind them was only getting louder as they moved deeper amongst the islands. Charles saw a small cluster of reptilians and a few humans atop a large island and knew it was where Marcos was. He couldn't explain exactly why he knew but it just felt like he was staring at the center of universe, a singular point where all things were made and unmade.

McDaniel halted their advance short of the island and they crept forward slowly until they reached its steep banks. McDaniel, slick with sweat and the blood of others, said quietly, "We have to be quick. Sarah is weakening greatly from all the exertion, though she is helped by the others she rescued. I can hear her thoughts. She is going to try and give us one more distraction and we can't lose time on it when it happens." Charles nodded his understanding and they slowly climbed the steep bank, which in their tired state was no simple feat. The bank was taller than both of them and slick with sticky mud that covered them both by the time they reached the top. They stayed low to the ground as they got as close as they dared.

Charles found a thick tree to hide behind and looked around with one eye to see what they faced at the center of the island. He peaked around then moved slowly back out of sight and said to McDaniel, "Five reptilians, including that white floating bastard. Also saw one bald human with them who was guarding Marcos's parents."

"And Marcos?" asked McDaniel, who was quickly clearing his barrel of mud with a small stick he found.

"He was kneeling before the white lizard. It appears to be holding his head in its claws."

"Fuck! They are doing the Ascending." McDaniel closed his eyes, "I have to tell Sarah to hurry." A few seconds passed as McDaniel remained unmoving, only the occasional contortion and grimace on his face showed he was not asleep. Charles became desperate as he could now clearly hear the weeping of Marcos's mother and the laughter of a human at her pain. McDaniel suddenly snapped back to the present but he appeared far wearier than before. "She and the others are spent or distracted. I can barely reach her now. She is too young and too weak to help us."

Charles looked around desperately, "What can we do? We will die pointlessly if we just rush them. Our pistols are not enough to slow down those reptiles before they reach and shred us." For the first time in the weeks he had gotten to know Colonel Nathan McDaniel, he saw hopeless loss on the man's face.

Marcos knelt before the Pale One, his head tilted back as he looked up at the inhuman beast, he had agreed to give himself to. Its long, boney arms were holding on to his shoulders as its eyes closed to concentrate. His head felt as if it were being crushed by the massive clawed hands that gripped tightly to him. He could see its chest heaving with heavy breathes, exposing ribs against its pale flesh. A migraine began to develop in his head as a new and unwelcomed sensation of himself being pulled into the Pale One's mind.

Marcos struggled to hold on to his own self and memories as he was flooded with the memories of the Pale One. He had memories of himself playing in his parent's backyard merged alongside a memory of snuggling warmly in a mud nest against a greenish reptilian, the Pale One's mother. On and on the memories leaked into each other, standing side by side at first then the human ones slowly being swept away. He no longer sat for hours in a brick school at a wooden desk, but instead had stood under a grove of trees before ancient, bent reptilians that showed him how to open rifts with his mind.

Marcos focused on these memories, struggling to gleam insight into more of the power. But the more he focused on the Pale One's memories, the more he felt his slip away. This mind wiping was not part of a normal Ascension, this was something new as it worked to totally remove him.

His concentration was broken by the feeling of his clawed hands digging into the frail, soft skinned creature before him. "NO!" He shouted in his mind as he realized he was letting his mind slip too much, feeling the Pale One's body and not his own.

At that moment he heard a voice saying, "Take me! Leave my son alone and take me!" His father was yelling but Marcos could not remember growing up with him. This man, who was his father, wanted to sacrifice himself in his stead. Amazing that someone he barely knew would do that for him, he thought. Marcos knew it was his own sacrifice to make and his alone. Marcos looked through the Pale One's memories again, feeling himself losing strength from the ordeal as the memories of who he was faded faster.

He found a memory of standing in an empty space, a rift with the bright light of sunshine coming through it next to him. He was in the First's realm at its conception. He watched as his own pale arms moved and waved as plants and water, islands and light started to fill the emptiness until it appeared a slice of the real world. He saw creation and how to do it.

Another memory took over, one of flame and smoke flying all around while he struggled to return to the realm as the world seemed to be burning. It was the asteroid hitting Earth. That was the great fear of the Pale One and he could see why. It was a nightmare vision of the end of the world.

The Pale One was focused on removing his memory and it was working. Marcos had lost all of his childhood and most of his teen years. It was as if he graduated from a place with no name and started working odd jobs to help his elderly parents make it through their days. *Marcos,* he thought. He had to keep repeating his own name for fear he would lose that too. He had to act fast now or nothing would be left of him. He reached out and felt those clawed hands again, wrapped around his head, and lifted them to the sky. He knew the Pale One noticed for it stopped trying to delete his memories and instead started to pull back from his body and back to its own. The struggle was bizarre for Marcos, a struggle to stay in an alien body as the alien entity savagely tried to unseat him. He only needed a single moment to form an image of what he wanted and then he could slip back to his body, which thankfully pulled on him as if a great rope pulled on him to return.

He succeeded and went whipping back to his own body. He opened his eyes and saw the Pale One still had its arms raised to the sky as it was momentarily frozen in horror at what was falling from above. Marcos looked up as the thick clouds in the sky parted in billowing waves as a massive meteor came hurtling down in the distance. The pale light of the swamp was replaced by a brilliant yellow and orange flame that cast long shadows on all. A guttural chittering started among the reptilians nearby as they looked and coward before the heavenly body that was plummeting toward them. Their shock was soon turned to absolute confusion as bullets started slamming into them. He looked

and saw McDaniel and Charles charging towards him firing

into the reptilians standing between them and the Pale One.

Marcos got to his feet and with one great leap,

jumped shoulder first into the midriff of the Pale One. He did

not know if it could reverse what he had done but he wasn't

waiting to find out. They landed together in a splash of mud

and the Pale One knocked him aside with one great swipe of

its left arm. Marcos rolled out of its way and saw briefly his

parents struggling with the bald man for the knife he had. He

got to his feet to jump on the Pale One, hoping to keep it

pinned and distracted when he felt the ground start to shake.

A massive earthquake was turning the mud into a liquid that

was starting to swallow everyone. He struggled to lift his legs

but it was hopeless. He looked up and no longer saw the fiery

meteor but his ears were suddenly assaulted by a tremendous

blast of air and pressure followed swiftly by black ash and

red-hot rock that flew through the air. Everything was going

black from the ash, and the wind and mud made him bend

over as he choked on scorching hot air. The Pale One

suddenly loomed before him and pulled him out of the mud and towards its open jaws. He thought, it's *going to bite my neck open!* But before it could happen, he felt two people moving alongside the Pale One, despite the fierce ash, and they pulled its head away from him. This caused all four of them to start to topple over. As Marcos watched them fall towards the mud, he saw a rift open beneath them and they all fell, spinning, into a concrete cafeteria room.

Ash, red hot pieces of rock, and burning wood came billowing in around them as they tumbled to the floor landing upon a plastic table with metal legs, shattering its frame. Marcos saw the world spin again as the Pale One heaved him over its head and he landed hard on his back, knocking all the air out of his lungs. He coughed painfully and saw ash fly out of his mouth in a disturbing amount. He rolled to his side and saw his saviors punching and wrestling with the Pale One. Colonel McDaniel, a huge man, was straddling the Pale One trying to hold its arms down as it bucked and kicked with razor sharp talons and claws. Charles had risen up and quickly was searching for something to pick up and hit it with.

"Quickly! I can't hold it!" shouted McDaniel. Just as he said this the Pale One grabbed his waist and lifted him into the air, getting its feet underneath him and raked its long taloned feet against his stomach. McDaniel's intestines and stomach spilled out onto the Pale One's feet as blood flowed out of his mouth and nose, choking off any words or screams he tried to make. Charles wrenched a long metal leg piece free of its attachment to the broken table, and quickly moved to stand over the Pale One. McDaniel, amazingly, was still holding on to the arms of the Pale One, keeping it from simply tossing him aside and getting up. Charles brought the metal bar down swiftly into the face of the Pale One, pulversing a green eyeball. He kept hitting it over and over again. Blood and brain matter arced through the air as he caved in its skull until it was dead.

Marcos had barely risen to his feet before Charles had crushed in the Pale One's skull. It had all happened in seconds. Several people in orange jumpsuits started to come to them and pulled McDaniel free of the reptilian but he was already dead. Sarah came running up to Charles and wrapped her arms around him.

"Don't look at it." Charles said as he went to cover her eyes. Sarah held his hand back and stared long at the dead.

"They deserved that. I had wished for it long ago." Her words were cold and unemotional but Marcos could see the rage inside this young girl at the monsters that lay dead before her.

Marcos stumbled as he made his way towards Charles and Sarah, debris littered the floor. "Open the rift again. We need to get my parents out."

Sarah shook her head slowly. "I tried to get them too but they were too far away and I was so spent. I am afraid to open it again. It is all burning and gone."

Marcos did not know how to react. He had called down the meteor himself. He had just murdered his parents along with anyone else that was there. His legs gave out and he fell to the floor hard. He looked up through blurry eyes at

Charles and Sarah. Charles was shouting at someone, waving them to help, but he could not hear. His ears were filled with a buzzing and his arms felt too weak to lift. He caught Charles's eye and said, "Tell me it was worth it." He saw Charles's lips moving but could not hear. His own words had sounded distant and muffled. A warmth was seeping into his body and an intense urge to sleep. He saw the panic in Sarah and Charles's eyes but didn't care. Nothing mattered it seemed. Peace settled over his mind as he drifted away.

Epilogue

One Month Later

Top-Secret Military Prison Delta Omega: Location Unknown

Charles Chenard walked the empty medical East Wing of the military prison Colonel Nathan McDaniel had been using to house captured individuals who had the power. People with abilities that had been awoken by the First and then used to unleash untold death and destruction across all of North America with the help of McDaniel's traitor elements in the U.S. Army. The First were defeated, Charles had killed the leader, the Pale One, who had also killed McDaniel. Without those two powerful individuals to guide the rebel forces the war had quickly petered out as mass surrenders took place.

Fear now ruled the land. The United Nations had sent in a globally run military to bring peace and stability to North America. The number one mission was to find and terminate all people known to have the power. It was open genocide as fear of these powers and the full realization of the reptilian First that had taken over many people's physical bodies. This existential horror drove the killings and allowed many to clear their consciences of what they were doing, after all, the reptilians were not human so likely anyone with the power was not either. Alien conspiracies ruled the airwaves as the media and experts poured fuel on the flames of fear.

Charles had stopped watching TV or reading news websites. He couldn't stand what he was seeing. He wasn't sure who had won as he watched people tear apart their friends and family members over fear they were not human. His mind leapt to an image of Marshall begging him to kill him as he was slowly turning into one of the First. Charles flinched at the memory. Was he no better? Did he not kill his own friend without trying to find a cure? He had thought there was no way to reverse it but yet he watched Marcos Ascend with the Pale One and comeback. Perhaps there had been a way but he had let fear drive him.

"Where the hell is everyone," Charles said out loud to himself. He hadn't seen a single person all morning. The prison was a massive facility with four main wings and there were only a little over fifty people left. Several had fled the prison at the time of the break out and all the guards and soldiers had been killed or placed in the First's realm. Still, the silence of the prison was setting him on edge.

He pushed into recovery room 215 where Marcos had been taken after he had lost consciousness. He did not wake for a week. Charles had been tortured by Marcos's final words, "Tell me it was worth it." During that week he had thought long and hard how to answer that. Still a month later he could not fully. Marcos had only allowed Sarah to visit him since he had awoken. But time was up for everyone soon and Charles had to see him. Had to find the words to answer the question that had been put upon him.

He opened the door and walked in to see Sarah sitting by an empty bed. She had found a large pair of grey sweat pants and a hoodie, that were both too large for her, in the locker room of the prison's gymnasium. She smiled as he walked in and he looked into the bathroom but it was dark and obviously empty. "Where is he?"

Sarah replied, "He has gone. He is working on a surprise. I'm waiting here for him to help him get back." Charles felt she was weird when he first met her but she only seemed to be getting weirder. He understood her though, she was an orphan and had been horribly traumatized for her young age.

"Gone? You mean he has gone back to the First's realm?! What the hell are you guys doing?!" Charles felt the ball of stress that had been in his stomach for months now starting to explode from even more insanity he was hearing. What madness would drive Marcos to go back? He thought of Marcos's poor parents that had tragically been left behind in that place and thought perhaps he was looking for them, what may be left of them.

Sarah tilted her head slightly and let out a light, airy laugh at his outburst. "No, not there. I am not sure anyone can go there again. The Pale One was its creator so without him it is lost if not destroyed." Charles felt relieved at the words but was now more puzzled than ever. Sarah seemed about to go on but suddenly she froze, much as McDaniel had when she would talk to him through their minds. She raised her hands and suddenly a black rift appeared on the other side of the bed and out stepped Marcos. Charles had expected a patient gowned and withered man but instead Marcos was wearing a prison guards grey khakis and button up cotton shirt, and physically looked rejuvenated.

Charles almost laughed seeing the man gingerly step out of the rift. He had only seen people tumble and fall from them, these two were mastering this power more and more. He also noticed that

Marcos looked strangely pleased and glowing, as if he had a hilarious secret that could make anyone smile.

"Charles, it is good to see you. Did you just get here?"

Charles paused at the causal words and nature of his friend. Charles moved closer to the two of them and said, "I just came in. What's going on? You are both a little too happy for this world."

A shadow crossed Marcos's face and Charles felt a twinge of regret at putting down happiness. It was all he hoped anyone would find and here he was begrudging it.

Marcos replied, "Yes, I agree. But we have something better than this world, and a way to save those with the power. I don't think we can stay here anymore."

Charles nodded, "Came here to say exactly that. It is time to move on. Won't be long before someone rats out our location to these new U.N. forces running the inquisition out there."

Marcos shook his head and replied, "We are not just moving on. We are leaving for good. I gained a lot from that pale reptilian. It may just have given back something good to us." The reality of what Marcos was saying finally dawned on Charles.

"Holy shit you didn't?" Charles exclaimed in surprise.

Sarah let out a tiny laugh, "Wait until you see it. Marcos is amazing, he is a real artist I think."

Marcos motioned with one hand and suddenly a void opened again. Beyond it, golden light shined through, along with the smell of summer flowers and fresh earth. The sound of a babbling creek and even bird song reached Charles's ears. He looked at Marcos with shocked surprise on his face. Marcos gave a slight gesture, motioning for Charles to go first. Charles stepped through and happily landed on both feet in a field of lush grass and yellow daisies. The small creek that cut through the meadow was only a few feet away from him and he could see fish jumping out to catch insects. He looked up and saw a flawless blue sky with a warm yellow sun shining down. Marcos was by his side, taking a deep breath of the warm air.

"This is amazing Marcos. You mean to take those with the power here?"

"Exactly. I have made everything I could think of to give us a good life here. A small village is on the other side of this river beyond those trees you see."

Charles looked back at the rift behind them. Sarah sat on the chair, inside the small medical room staring at them, her gentle smile beaming back at him. "So, you bring them all here but what then? What are you going to do here?"

"We wait," Marcos paused as he stared deeply into the rushing creek. "We wait until Earth can take us back or has forgotten what has happened. We won't age here. Much like the First's realm we are standing outside of time and space."

"But you saw what had become of them. The First's realm must have looked like this at first. Sunshine and green trees. But eventually…"

Marcos spoke softly, finishing his friend's sentence. "Eventually it decayed along with their minds, I know. We all just need peace now Charles. Haven't we earned some peace." Charles saw tears form in Marcos's eyes and thought back again to the question.

"Marcos, before you passed out you asked me to tell you it was worth it." Marcos looked cautiously at him, a fear of hearing a truth he might not want in his eyes. Charles could clearly see that fear and knew it well. "There is no answer to that, not one we can know. We got swept up in something beyond our control and dealt with it in the moment the best we could. I am sorry about your parents, but know that it wasn't you that brought them into that place. Their deaths are on McDaniel and the Pale One. And them alone. All deaths are on them." A flash of Marshall's slumped and bleeding body crossed his mind, sending an unbidden tear down his face.

Marcos smiled a sad smile at him. "Thank you, Charles. I needed that." He looked away again and took another deep breath. "Charles, I have already brought everyone through. They are already at the village, not a single one refused to come here. And, now Charles I have to ask you. Will you join us?"

Charles felt his first reaction of joy at the thought of being in this Eden, but suppressed it as best he could. He saw that Marcos noticed the joy in his eyes, but he felt wrong about it. He started to back away, back towards the rift. "I can't Marcos. I'm not worth all this."

A soft voice spoke behind him, "What do you mean? Of course, you are." He turned to see Sarah standing in the meadow, her baggy clothes making her look even younger than she was. She walked softly across the tall grass and held his hand in hers. "This is the best way, for all of us."

Charles slowly pulled his hand from hers and backed up again towards the rift. Their puzzled and saddened faces cut deeply into him. Sarah appeared to falter and shook her head. She said in a strained voice, "I can't keep it open much longer. Marcos is helping me but even he can't match what the Pale One allowed me to do for all those years. Please come with us."

Charles was only a few steps from the wavering rift. "Marcos, I'm not worthy of this. I... I can't forgive myself for what I have done."

Marcos's face pulled tightly into a pained expression. "You and me both. But punishing yourself will not make it better."

"I killed Marshall. I shot him dead instead of finding some way to save him." Charles was shaking from the words. He could barely stand to say them. "I let him down and became no better than McDaniel."

Marcos walked to him and grabbed him by his upper arms and said, "I saw Marshall Ascend. He couldn't have been saved by you. In time you can tell me exactly what happened but for now it is done. Put him to rest and forgive yourself. This is also, McDaniel and the Pale One's doing. Just like all the other deaths."

Charles looked into the earnest, bright brown eyes of Marcos and saw a new man before him. Wiser and less afraid than he had been before. He nodded and heard a sigh of relief from Sarah as the rift closed behind them.

Charles turned and saw only more open fields toward rolling hills where the rift had been. "Is there no one out there to let us back into the real world?"

Marcos replied, "They are out there. And when the world changes we will go back. But now we need to let it pass." He paused in contemplation then said, "At first I couldn't remember anything that had happened to me before I was eighteen, the Pale One had started to try and erase my memories. Now the memories have slowly returned, I suppose nothing is gone forever and nothing is forever hopeless. People will change and we will get a second chance."

Charles considered him for a moment then replied, "The First wanted a second chance too." He did not mean his words to be an argument, merely an observation that came blurting out.

Marcos nodded and started off towards the woods where the village was. "True, but they had hoped for a return to the past. We are just waiting on the future." Charles felt the first bit of hope enter him in a longtime. He reached out for Sarah's hand and they walked across a shallow part of the river and towards the sound of laughter coming from the village beyond the woods.

www.ingramcontent.com/pod-product-compliance
Lightning Source LLC
Chambersburg PA
CBHW051957150726
47999CB00004B/1416